BIN BOY

TOM VAUGHAN

ILLUSTRATED BY EMMA McCANN

■ SCHOLASTIC

Published in the UK by Scholastic Children's Books, 2021
Euston House, 24 Eversholt Street, London, NW1 1DB, UK
A division of Scholastic Limited.

London – New York – Toronto – Sydney – Auckland
Mexico City – New Delhi – Hong Kong

SCHOLASTIC and associated logos are trademarks and/or
registered trademarks of Scholastic Inc.

ISBN 978 0702 30528 3

A CIP catalogue record for this book is available
from the British Library.

Printed by CPI Group (UK) Ltd, Croydon, CR0 4YY
Papers used by Scholastic Children's Books are made
from wood grown in sustainable forests.

1 3 5 7 9 10 8 6 4 2

www.scholastic.co.uk

To Dad – T.V.

To Dylbo Baggins. Who is pretty
super himself – E.M.

CHAPTER 1

Holidaying in a Hollowed-Out Volcano

I'm Billy Benbow. I'm ten years old. And I HATE holidaying in a hollowed-out volcano.

Bet you can't say *that* quickly.

"I hate hollowing in a holiday volcano!"

See? It's super hard.

"I hate hollowdaying in a holly-out volcano!"

Even *I* can't do it. And I've been trying for the past two weeks, pretty much non-stop, to anyone who would listen: my mum, my stepdad . . . his henchmen.

It was the last day of the school holidays, and I was

inside, you guessed it . . . a hollowed-out volcano. That's right: an actual volcano located somewhere off the coast of Hawaii, I think. It's extinct now and pimped up into a gazillion-pound holiday home by my stepdad, Phil. You probably think that sounds really cool, but I hate it more than homework. No: make that doing homework while drinking PholaCola . . . but we'll get to that last bit. Luckily, my best friend, Viv, came to the volcano to keep me company. And he is smart enough to beat any tongue-twister.

"You – hate – holidaying – in – a – hollowed – out – volcano!" he said, his black eyebrows bouncing over his glasses as he pronounced each word.

I screwed my face up and tried one last time: "I HATE hollering in a holy day volcano . . . o . . . o . . . o . . . o!"

The "o" echoed around the volcanic walls of my bedroom, finally dying out with a little squeak in the corner. I admitted defeat and we both fell back into silence on my bed, bored out of our brains. Hollowed-out holiday volcanoes might look cool, but they are boring as hell.

Above us, the brown rock of the volcano wall met the shiny chrome ceiling, and there was a faint smell of egg that was either volcanic gases or Viv's breath.

The silence only ended when Viv slurped down the last drops of PholaCola from his can, then internalized a burp that looked like a grenade going off inside his mouth. His eyes looked panicked, darting side to side as the blast lasted about a month. When it finally finished, he said: "Let's go ask Phil for more PholaCola!" and held the empty can in front of my face. "Maybe he's got a PholaCola swimming pool?"

Viv might be smart, but he has got one weakness: he'll do *anything* for some disgusting PholaCola. Actually, he has two weaknesses: there is also his overactive imagination. Who's ever heard of a swimming pool filled with cola? Not that Viv is a good swimmer anyway... *Actually*, he has three weaknesses: his weakness is also a weakness. He is about as strong as a baby vole. Which is what makes him such a target for bullies. Not that I can talk. I'm not sure who gets picked on more: Viv or me. But we'll get to all of that.

I rolled my eyes and fell back further on to my bed.

"Urgh. Do we *have* to? You *know* I hate being around Pheel."

Phil (or *Pheel* as I call him, just to be annoying) is my new stepdad. And if there's one thing I hate more than holidaying in a hollowed-out volcano, it's my stepdad, Pheel.

"Come on, *pleeaaaaasssseee!*" The echo made Viv sound desperate. I looked him up and down as his eyes bulged with another internal burp. The levels of CO_2 in his bloodstream must be close to toxic. If I poked him, he'd probably explode. I don't know why he liked PholaCola so much; it tasted like cough syrup. But then again, I was pretty much the only person in the world who thought that.

I looked around my vast, empty bedroom. Then I looked at Viv's pleading, desperate face. I couldn't resist him, even if he was slowly morphing from a human form into a fizzy gas.

"All right. But let's be quick. Pheel's always so . . . annoying."

Viv bounced off my bed and punched the air. We set off across my room. My door slid open with a futuristic *swoosh* and we hopped on the monorail. I pushed a button that said BOARDROOM and we sped off through the volcano-plex.

"How do you not get excited by all of this?" said Viv, craning his neck as we whizzed through a lava tube dripping with giant stalactites. He loves it here. That's because it's like he's inside a giant school project, which is probably a fantasy of his.

I fixed my eyes straight ahead. "Why would I get excited about having to hang out with Pheel?"

Ever since my mum got remarried to Pheel last year, my life has got about five hundred times worse. First, it's like I'm suddenly invisible to Mum. Second, all the kids at school have started to notice me (and that's not a good thing). And third, I have to spend far too much time around fake, smarmy Pheel, doing things like going to his stupid hollowed-out holiday volcano. It might look impressive, but it is *so* boring – just endless rock corridors and locked rooms. Everyone else at school's parents take them to Center Parcs or Disneyland. And, to make it doubly better for them, their parents aren't Pheel.

We whooshed around a corner. Beneath us, a

heatproof window displayed a long drop into the bottomless magma chamber.

"How'd he even *afford* this?" asked Viv, his mouth hanging so far open you could fit a cow in it.

I kept my eyes dead ahead as the monorail lurched right, and replied, "By making billions inventing that disgusting drink you love."

The monorail pulled to a sudden stop, throwing us forwards. "YOU HAVE ARRIVED AT THE BOARDROOM," said a clipped female voice out of a little speaker on the control panel. We were in a long corridor that stretched for what seemed like miles in both directions. Its walls were bare rock face, and long silver ventilation shafts tracked the ceiling. Viv coughed and its echo bounced down, down, down the corridor until it disappeared. In front of us towered a metal door. Thick yellow-and-black striped lines flanked the frame and a red bulb flashed above it. Maybe to say: "DON'T GO IN". Or maybe just to add a nice lighting effect. Who was I to know? More to the point: Who was I to care?

Viv's eyes bulged with a sudden panic. "Can we go in? The red light's on!"

"Dunno, let's find out," I said with a shrug.

"But the red light's flashing! Surely that means 'Don't go in'?" Viv sounded his usual panicky self and he was hiccuping like a cartoon drunk. The last thing he needed was more fizzy drink, but he was his own boss.

"Maybe. Probably. Who cares?" I said, pulling out my key card and bleeping it against the lock, more in hope than expectation. A siren gave off a loud "BARP!" and the same cold female voice sounded from ceiling speakers: "BOARDROOM UNLOCKED. BOARDROOM UNLOCKED."

"Well, what do you know?" I said, shrugging in surprise. Viv's eyes widened and he started sweating heavily. He's my best friend and all – and he is hands down the smartest person I know – but *boy* is he a wimp.

The metal doors glided apart to reveal the cathedral-sized boardroom full of people ...

very *odd-looking* people. They were all sitting around a big circular table in the middle of the room like it was some super-important meeting. Above them, a huge holographic map of the world rotated through the air, with the words "GLOBAL DOMINATION PLAN" stretched across it in holographic text.

As per usual, no one seemed to notice me. Sometimes it's like I'm freakin' invisible.

"Erm, hi, everyone," I said loudly.

Immediately, the room was filled with the sound of coughing, papers being ruffled and chair legs scraping along the floor. The holographic globe crackled and vanished.

"Billy! Erm, what are you doing here, buddy?"

Urgh. There he was. *Pheel*. Phil. Phileas Pern. My *stepdad*. I hated even using the word "dad" with him. Almost as much as I hated his bright-white fake grin, his groomed ginger beard, and his obsession with purple suits. Like a flash, he was on his feet and pivoting around the table. "I didn't know you could get in here! How did you get in here?" he asked, forcing a smile that didn't disguise his anxious eyes.

"Mum gave me a pass," I replied, coldly waving my key card at him. "Can we get another PholaCola from the kitchen?"

He was in front of me now, blocking my view of the room, subtly trying to usher me towards the door. I refused to budge, peering around him at the cast of weird characters at the table. And when I say weird, I mean *weird*. Beef-ice-cream weird. Marry-a-cat weird. There was a hulking woman with curly blonde hair and a green weightlifter's leotard; an angular, metallic robot; a whippet-thin woman dressed in fur; and a

disembodied brain in a jar that was wired up to a laptop. There must have been ten or twelve of them in total, each as odd-looking as the next.

"Who's the brainy dude?" I asked, nodding at the grey matter in the jar.

Pheel looked over his shoulder briefly and crinkled his forehead. "These are my friends and colleagues and we're just ... um ... practising our Halloween costumes. Yes! That's it!"

"But it's May," I replied, narrowing my eyes.

Pheel was unusually flustered. "Sure. It's never too early to, you know, brainstorm..." He winced at the turn of phrase. "I mean workshop! Never too early to workshop ideas." He looked over his shoulder at the brain in a jar and muttered, "No offence meant, Lord Krung."

The brain in a jar replied through a laptop, in the kind of weird electronic voice you get when you make a computer read your homework out loud. "**NONE TAKEN**."

I scanned the room. Everyone was grinning nervously at me.

"*Aaaaaaaaanyway,*" I said, still watching them from

the corner of my eye. "Viv wants *another* PholaCola." I glanced behind me at my best friend. He was standing in the corridor, white as a sheet and trembling. He's not great with new people.

"Of course you can get a PholaCola! The PholaCola's free! Have as much PholaCola as you like!" said Pheel at the speed of light. He took another step forward and tried to use his body to edge me out of the room. He must have been hot in his horrible purple suit, because I saw a single bead of sweat trickle down his forehead.

I held my ground. "What exactly are you all *doing* in here?"

There was more coughing, and everyone exchanged sideways glances. Finally the awkward silence was broken when a small, wrinkled man stood up and shuffled towards me, a twisted smile painted on his gaunt, pale face. His leather-gloved hands hung limply in front of a starched white lab coat and he wore a pair of round steel-framed glasses, enlarging eyes that were like black marbles.

"You must be the Billy I hear so much about!" he said in a reedy German accent. "May I introduce myself; I am Professor Ernst Furds, the new managing director of PholaCola!"

I frowned. "Did you say Farts?"

"Furds," he repeated.

"Farts?" I recapped.

"F-uh-ds," he said, the humour draining from his black eyes.

"Fuds. Got it. Sorry, it's just your accent. . ." I shook his cold, floppy hand.

"Not to worry, boy. You must please call me the Professor – everyone does!" He held out an unopened can of PholaCola. "Here, your friend must have my own PholaCola!" He attempted to pop it open, but the ring pull was too tough for his puny fingers. Finally, in a fit of anger, he placed it on the table and clapped twice. One of a dozen or so manservants stepped out from the shadows at the edge of the room.

(That's another annoying thing about *Pheel* – you can't go *anywhere* without there being about twenty manservants clad all in black, hovering around silently. I nickname them *henchmen*, just to annoy Pheel.)

Almost robotically, the henchman popped the top

off the cola and handed it back to the Professor. Then he clasped his hands behind his back and reversed stealthily into the shadows.

The Professor passed me the opened can. "Your stepfather has made a most impressive drink!" he said, then rubbed his withered hands together and smiled, his thin purple tongue licking his chapped lips. "We are just . . . perfecting the formula!"

The rest of the room burst out in muffled guffaws. Even the brain laughed through its laptop. "**HA. HA. HA.**"

Pheel cleared his throat like an unhappy schoolteacher. The laughs morphed into fake coughs. The Professor quickly changed the subject. "It must be most fun coming on holiday to this volcano, no?"

I shrugged indifferently, but Pheel jumped in before I could answer.

"Well, we need to kit it out a bit, don't we, Billy? It's still a bit of a bachelor pad at the moment. It needs some games consoles, paintball course, that kind of thing."

He was forcibly ushering me towards the door now. I could feel his thighs push into me as he edged me backwards. I took another step back and found myself by the monorail.

"Anyway, sorry, buddy, but business is pressing, gotta go. Let's catch up later." He repeatedly hammered a button beside the doors and the Professor gave a limp wave as they swooshed shut. A "BARP!" of the siren signalled the room had relocked.

I turned to Viv and handed him the PholaCola. "Here you go." He was white as a sheet and trembling. I retracted it. "You know what, I think you've had enough."

His teeth were chattering and he was trying to say something. He'd either gone cold turkey on the cola front or he'd been spooked by a bunch of very early Halloween costumes. After about a minute, he finally spat his sentence out. "W-w-what did you say your stepdad does again?"

"You know what he does," I replied. "He's the founder of PholaCola, the drinks company."

Viv took a moment to compose himself. "You know the other day when I joked that your stepdad is probably a supervillain or something if he owns a hollowed-out volcano?"

I lowered my eyelids and replied: "Yeah. I remember."

He looked at me with unflinching intensity. "Well. . . Did you see that room??? I think your stepdad IS a supervillain! I think they are ALL supervillains!"

What did I tell you about Viv's imagination? I put a hand on his shoulder reassuringly. "Buddy – those were a bunch of Halloween costumes! That's what billionaires do – stupid, pointless stuff that no one understands." I reached behind me and placed his PholaCola in a nearby rubbish bin. "Come on, supervillains only exist in your comic books. Don't be a cliché. Now, let's get on the monorail, head back through the hollowed-out volcano and go to bed. It's the first day of term tomorrow and we've got a long trip back home in the morning."

CHAPTER 2
The Alps?

Turns out it's not such a long trip home if your stepdad owns his own souped-up purple Concorde. We left before breakfast and were home well before school started. Viv was so excited about the way the Concorde's nose levered up and down that Pheel even let him poke his head out of the window for the landing, which left his hair sticking up like a giant black Dorito. It also left him acting pretty wired and skittish for the day. Or that could have been the four PholaColas he had with his in-flight breakfast.

He was still acting intense when he leaned over to me during the final class of the day – history with Mr

Meringue – and whispered: "It said 'Global Domination Plan' above the holographic globe!"

"Of course it did!" I hissed back. "He runs an international drinks company!"

"And all those weirdo supervillains around the table!" he whispered.

"They were *Halloween* costumes!" I hissed. "Trust me. If anyone wants to believe that Pheel is a supervillain, or even just a shoplifter, it's me. Mum would dump him straight away. But it's fantasy!"

He looked away and sighed dramatically through his nostrils. "I can't believe you don't see it."

"I can't believe you have a burrito bean stuck in the gap between your front teeth!" I retorted.

Flustered, he took off his glasses and squinted into the reflection, looking for the non-existent bean.

"Where? I can't see!" he whispered.

"Now!" piped up Mr Meringue. "Who can tell me who the biggest, baddest baddie was during this time?"

I snapped back into the lesson and tried to remember what it was about.

Dorothy Wagon put her hand up. "Is it E-numbers, Mr Meringue? My mum says it's E-numbers."

Whatever the answer was, I was fairly certain it wasn't that.

Mr Meringue tried to disguise a frown. "No, Dorothy. I meant the biggest baddie in 1920s America. This is a *history* lesson."

She put her hand down and continued licking her crayons.

Viv's hand shot up. "Is it Al Capone, sir?"

"Yes, Viv! I can always rely on you." He galloped over to Viv's desk and gave him a high five with an embarrassingly angular elbow. The two of them had a weird thing going on.

"A real-life *supervillain*, if you will! And can anyone tell me who defeated him?" He scanned the room. "Come on, team! Who orchestrated his arrest? It *is* a tough one. . . No. . .?" He trotted back to the whiteboard, his patterned, knitted tank top bouncing with each step, and scrawled across it. "E-L-I-O-T N-E-S-S. Eliot Ness. A real-life *superhero*, if you will! Just an ordinary man who took down one of the worst men in history!"

A huge roar and screech from outside the window broke my attention. I closed my eyes and my heart sank. I didn't need to look to know who had arrived. Another of the worst men in history. Pheel was pulling up in his rocket car.

Everyone gasped in excitement and started whispering.

"Phil Pern's here!"

"I can't wait to see his car again!"

"I hope he's brought free drinks!"

People think it must be the coolest thing ever to have a billionaire stepdad, like it's all premium ice cream and indoor archery. But not when it's *Pheel*. I've tried to like the guy. Honestly I have. And it's not just that he's really fake and cringey and show-offy. It's the stuff that I notice that no one else does. Like the way he pretends like he wants to do stuff with me when really it's just an act to impress Mum. Or the way he looks at other kids' mums when he picks me up. Or the way he thinks he can buy his way out of any problem. Or the way he's just not my dad. But my real dad died three years ago. And now my mum is with Pheel. So, I guess I'm stuck with him. But it doesn't mean I have to like it.

The school bell rang and the class jumped up as one, crowding around the window to get a look at Pheel's rocket car.

"How can a loser like you have such a cool stepdad like Phil Pern?" belched Brayden Balls, spit flying from his slobbery big lips. "He obviously can't be your REAL dad." Then he laughed and pressed his face against the window like he was a gorilla at the zoo.

And that's the other thing Pheel does ... he makes my life a million times worse. If it wasn't for him, I could just slip by under the radar with nothing to draw attention to me. Instead, he's just a constant loud reminder that I'm not as try-hard cool as him. And, as far as I can tell, try-hard cool is the only thing that wins you friends.

I turned from the window to see Mr Meringue fly through the door, his trilby hat on his head and raincoat hung over one arm. And then – BLAM! – my world was plunged into darkness.

"Ha ha! Billy Bin Boy!" came the tinny taunt.

"Har-de-ha!" I said, yanking the bin off my head. "Why don't you do something original for a change?"

"OK!" Brayden did a fart noise under his armpit while the rest of the class pointed and laughed at me. I wiped bin juice from my hair, slung my backpack over a shoulder and marched out to the tune of "Baa, Baa, Black Sheep" played in armpit fart.

I swallowed down the lump in my throat. I could hear Viv panting as he ran to catch up with me.

"You know what my dad says – just rise above it," he

said, breathlessly.

I nodded and strode on. I wish I had a dad to give me advice. Pheel just looks embarrassed when someone brings up bullying. I sucked down my self-pity and bottled it up deep inside. Then I burst open the school doors and recoiled. Pheel was in his purple suit and sunglasses, lolling on the bonnet of his rocket car, handing out cans of PholaCola to a mob of clamouring schoolkids. Urgh. *Such* a try-hard.

I said a quick "See you later" to Viv, hunched my shoulders and marched across the playground.

"Hey-hey, Billy!" he said, looking up and firing me a finger pistol. He's always extra fake when people are watching. "Mum's busy feeding the pets – so I said I'd do the school run in the rocket car. Cool, hey?" He pulled his sunglasses down his nose and flashed me a wink.

"Sure. Let's go," I said, pulling the passenger-door handle. It hissed and levered open, and I climbed in.

He turned to the mob of kids slurping on cans of his horrible cola and flashed a peace sign. "Later, gang. And remember – have a PholaCola Kinda Day!"

They screamed like he was a pop star leaving a stadium. A couple of girls had PholaCola streaming out of their nostrils. Another boy had taken his top off and was swinging it around his head, his belly flab jiggling with a hypnotic wobble. People go mad for his drink. . . I don't get it.

The doors closed and I slumped into my seat. In front of me, on the dashboard, sat what looked like a crumpled silk handkerchief. Except it had a couple of big holes in it and was tied in a bow. Pheel saw me clock it. Quick as a flash he reached across, snatched it and stuffed it guiltily in his pocket. I'd be like that too if I left my dirty hanky lying around. In its place I chucked my schoolbooks.

"Not there! The metal spines scratch the mahogany!" snapped Phil before he could check himself. Then he quickly tried to bury his annoyance with a fake smile and a heavy dose of try-hard. "Just chuck 'em in the back! Who cares about schoolwork, huh? I never did!" He thumbed over his shoulder and pushed his sunglasses back on to the bridge of his nose. And with that, the usual awkward atmosphere descended inside the car. The clamour from outside the window seemed like a different universe.

"Good day at school?" asked Pheel, with a smile that pretended to care, as he opened up the throttle.

"It was all riiiiiiiiiiiiiiiiiiiiiiiiiiiiiiiiiiiiiiiiight," I replied, my skull forced into the headrest as the rocket jets kicked in.

"Glllllllllaaaaaaaaaaaaaaaddddddddddd tooooooooooooo heeeeeeeeeeaaaaaaaaaaaarrrrrrrrrrrr iiiiiiitttttttttttt," said Pheel as we reached terminal velocity. We tore down the middle of the road and he looked across at me with a bright white, self-satisfied smile, assuming I'd be impressed by the car. I wasn't. The crease lines that appeared in the corners of his eyes told me that he knew it. However hard he tried, however much he put on the cool-guy persona, he couldn't avoid the unspoken secret between us: we both knew it was all an act. The smile; the clothes; the desperation to look cool. And if it all fell away, there'd be nothing of him left.

We sped on in awkward silence, whizzing past motorcyclists like they were tiny planets on our intergalactic voyage. Pheel wasn't saying anything, but his face looked like it was trying harder than ever. Like he wanted to say something but didn't know how. Finally, when the G-forces levelled out, he spat it out.

"Hey. How'd you like to start again?" he asked.

I pulled a face. "No thanks. I don't really like fast cars."

"No, I mean how'd you like to start again *in life*? You know – a do-over?"

"A do-over?"

"Yeah," he continued. "Somewhere new. A fresh start somewhere different."

I looked at him from the corner of my eye. "Like, where?"

"Oh, I don't know . . . maybe . . . the Alps?" His voice rose up at the end of the sentence with a fragile hope.

"The Alps?" I shout-snorted.

"Yes. The Alps." He was sounding more confident now, like this was no longer a suggestion. "Me, your mum . . . you. A new start in the Alps." He looked at me over his sunglasses. "What do you say?"

If it wasn't for the considerable effects of the G-force,

I would have made a scene. But I was pinned back in my seat. Inside, though, I was FURIOUS! Move away from the town I'd grown up in? Where I'd lived with Dad? Move away from Viv? From everything and everyone I knew? To what – some remote complex at the top of a snowy mountain. No freaking way!

"The Alps??? Are you mad?" I finally spluttered.

"No. Well, I hope not." He took a second to check himself in the rear-view mirror. "I have an awesome mountain complex that I would love to be our new start. A *do-over* for us . . . for you, especially."

My anger turned from hot to freezing cold. "Why do I *'especially'* need a do-over?" I asked between gritted teeth.

He looked at me and tried to disguise a look that said: Are you being thick? "You know, buddy: it's just that you have a rotten time at school and perhaps you need to toughen up. Some time in the mountains would be good for you, hey?"

Rotten time? Toughen up? Mountains?

"I don't need to toughen up!" I shouted, the rocket-powered brakes now throwing me forward. "What leads you to that conclusion, *Sherlock*?"

He looked down at my jumper and said, matter-of-factly, "You have a banana skin on your shoulder."

"I KNOW!" I shouted, glancing down in surprise at the bin residue. "It's a new fashion style!"

We screeched down the drive towards Pheel's enormous garage, pulling to a halt alongside his hovercraft and a purple Chinook helicopter he called the PholaCopter. The

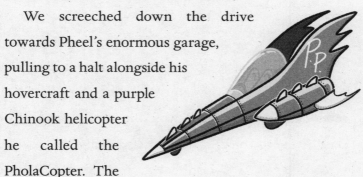

engine died with a soft hum and Pheel said: "Come on, Billy! You're letting the world walk over you and I just want to help. You're in danger of becoming a lo . . . lo . . . lo. . ." He was about to say "loser". I knew it. He knew it. I felt the ice freezing in my veins. ". . .lost cause," he finally spat out, which wasn't much better. He tried to disguise a wince.

Pulsing with icy rage, I popped the handle and the car door levered open.

"Yeah? Well, my REAL dad loved me for who I

was!" I shouted as I clambered from the rocket car.
"And there's no way I'm going to the Alps with you and
neither is Mum!"

And with that, I slammed the door and stormed up
to my bedroom.

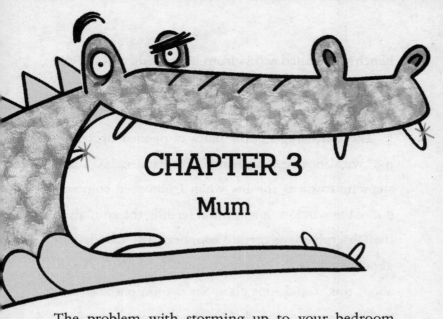

CHAPTER 3
Mum

The problem with storming up to your bedroom when you live in a five-floor decommissioned purple observatory (which Pheel calls the Obserphatory) is that it takes *ages*. I was knackered by the time I'd climbed the stone staircase to the front door. But I was still furious.

I can't believe Pheel nearly called me a loser!

I can't believe Mum married him!

I can't believe I had to leave the home we lived in with Dad and move into Pheel's stupid Obserphatory!

I kicked the huge wooden door in frustration and let out a little yelp when it refused to budge. A suit-clad henchman leaned across from his posting and twisted the handle.

"Thanks," I muttered.

The glistening marble hallway opened up before me, with its sweeping hand-carved staircases. I was stepping towards the lift when I glimpsed someone out of the window. It was Mum feeding the animals in the Obserphatory's private zoo, her curly blonde hair glowing gold in the afternoon sun. She needed to know about this stupid Alps plan. She'd soon put a stop to it. There was no way she'd agree to move away from Blemish, our hometown.

I marched out of the stained-glass patio doors, across the giant courtyard and down the zigzag stairs to the zoo. Below me, Blemish lay in neat lines like grids on graph paper. When I was younger, this was a crumbling, disused observatory. Then Pheel launched PholaCola. Now it lords it over the town like a sultan's palace, its bottling plant spewing out sweet-scented cola clouds that you can almost taste on the air as they roll and tumble over the town. Even his smell follows me around.

I reached the bottom of the stairs and marched past the man-eating-wolves enclosure, pulling up beside a sign that read GIANT KILLER NILE CROCODILES. Below me, in the pen, a green soup of stagnant-smelling water was broken only by the occasional pair of cold eyes. Mum stood on a sandy verge, a bucket full of meat by her feet, facing down an ENORMOUS chained-up crocodile.

"Just feeding Dennis here!" she called. "He's been a bit off his food. So I'm hand-feeding him."

Mum loved nursing: whether it was people, animals or prehistoric human-eating reptiles. She saw the good in everyone. Even crocodiles. *Even* Pheel.

I hurried down the steps and on to the sand.

"Mum, you need to know something!" I panted. "Pheel is plotting to move us to the Alps!"

"Call him by his proper name, sweetie," said Mum, tossing Dennis a hunk of steak.

"Phil. That's what I said," I panted. "Pheel is planning

on moving us to the Alps."

"I know, darling," she replied, catching me completely by surprise.

"What? Why didn't you tell me?" I spluttered.

She looked down, giving me those everything-will-be-fine eyes that make her such a great nurse. "I would have, sweetie, but Phil wanted to tell you himself. He's really excited about it!"

"Excited?! Well, I'll tell you who's not excited – me! I'm not going to leave Viv and Blemish and go and live on the top of some mountain!"

She pursed her lips, just like she does when she's ripping off a plaster – when I know that she feels sorry for me but is pretending it won't hurt.

"Viv can come visit any time you want," she replied, and tossed Dennis more steak. He snapped it up with a terrifying "pop", and I noticed that something about his mouth didn't look quite right.

"That's not the point, Mum! Pheel can't just tell us what to do!"

She tucked a loose strand of curly hair behind her ear. "He's not telling us what to do, sweetie. I thought it was a good idea as well. I like the mountains. And I think it would help you bond with Phil. It'll be an adventure!"

She lobbed some more meat at Dennis and I finally clocked what was bugging me about his mouth. "Has Dennis got . . . metal teeth?"

Mum smiled. "Yes, he has. Phil saw that all the giant crocs were getting plaque so he bought them all false teeth . . . made of pure platinum. He's such a softy like that!"

"This is what I mean about Pheel!" I said, stomping my foot. "He thinks he can buy himself out of any situation!"

"But, sweetie, he *can* buy himself out of any situation." She fished out the last chunk of steak, lobbing it into Dennis's mouth, where it disappeared with a ferocious snap of his metallic teeth, and continued: "But there was a time when he wasn't rich; a time when he had giant killer crocodiles with normal teeth. There might even have been a time when he didn't have giant killer crocs at all; just regular ones. Perhaps that he kept in a big fish tank or something; I don't know. But the point is – he's worked hard for all of this. And he deserves to have giant killer crocs with whatever kind of teeth he wants. He's a good man."

Like I say, Mum always sees the good in people. It's lovely and all, but when it comes to Pheel it is *sooo* infuriating.

I pulled a face. "There's something not right about him. . ." I muttered under my breath.

Mum shot me a "not again" look. "We've gone over this, Billy. Everyone in this town loves Phil. Would they do that if there was something *'not right'* about him?"

I crossed my arms and looked away. This wasn't going how I'd expected. How could Mum side with *Pheel* over me? My gaze wandered angrily over the town, looking at the school, at Viv's house, at all the things I'd leave behind. Finally they settled on a little patch of green on the far side of town – the graveyard where we buried Dad. A painful thought hit me – Dad would think we were abandoning him! "But what about Dad? We can't leave Dad behind!" I said, pointing to his little patch of green.

Mum closed her eyes, as if the words pained her.

Then she crouched down and took hold of my hand, speaking softly and calmly: "I loved your dad with all my heart." She paused for a second in thought, then continued: "But he would understand that there comes a time when you've got to move on with your life. And that doesn't mean that what went before doesn't count."

Her gaze swallowed me in warmth, briefly melting my anger.

"I know you struggle accepting Phil. And that's only to be expected. But he really does love us. Soon you'll see that. And then everything will be OK, I promise. He'll never be your proper dad, and he doesn't *want* to replace him. But he does want the same thing that Dad did – he wants the best for me and you."

Before I could say anything, she'd pulled me in for a hug that was so tight that there was no way you'd get a ruler between us, let alone Pheel. I found myself hoping that it would never end. After a moment, she gave a little sigh and said: "I'm afraid I've got to be going. I'm working nights."

She let go and I got a sudden uncontrollable feeling that we were growing apart. I had to do something about it. "Let's talk about the Alps tomorrow after school!" I said, with just a hint of desperation. "Maybe we can play Scrabble all evening like we used to after Dad d. . ." I trailed off and Mum's apologetic eyes told me all I needed to know.

"I'm so sorry, sweetie, but Phil's opening the new wing of that children's hospital he paid for. It's important I go."

Of course: *Pheel*. Pheel comes first. Or at least, he seems to these days.

She brushed put her hand on my cheek and said: "How about the next day?"

I shrugged and mumbled, "Sure," as she headed up the steps to the Obserphatory.

And with that, she was gone, leaving me standing alone in a zoo enclosure with a platinum-toothed crocodile who wanted nothing more than to bite my head off and eat it like a giant Ferrero Rocher. Finally, my frustration bubbled over and I shouted after her: "I'm important too, you know!"

But I don't know if she heard.

CHAPTER 4
Supervillain Checklist.
Tick. Tick. Tick.

"The Alps?!" said Viv.

"The Alps," I replied.

"But we'll never see each other!" he said.

I tried to put a brave face on it. "You'll meet other friends."

We looked out from our normal position, hiding behind the bins, and surveyed the rest of the playground. We both knew it wasn't true.

"We've got to stop it!" he said. "How do we stop it?"

"There's only one thing we can do: break up Mum and Pheel," I replied.

Viv nodded, and then I could sense the cogs in his brain whirring: "Let's make a plan."

That's the thing about Viv: he might be a giant wimp with an overactive imagination, but he's got one hell of a brain on him. And boy, can he cook up a good plan.

He opened his notebook and scrawled. "PLAN TO BREAK UP BILLY'S MUM AND PHIL"

Then he thought, and added:

"(SO THAT BILLY DOESN'T HAVE TO MOVE TO THE ALPS.)"

He added four exclamation marks, underlined it and, finally, sucked the top of his pen triumphantly. We unfurled a Ribena each and took a sweet slurp.

"We need your mum to see once and for all what a dork he is," said Viv, getting ready to write. "Let's list some of his dork qualities."

I didn't blink before answering: "He's fake, needy, irritating, try-hard, show-offy, thinks he can solve everything with money, tries to act really young, stares at other mums in the playground, picks his teeth and thinks I'm a loser," I said. Viv scrawled them down, then left his pen poised above the page.

"Anything else?" he said, raising an eyebrow.

I thought for a second. "He drinks straight from the milk bottle."

I could tell it wasn't what Viv wanted to hear. "No. Anything *else*?"

I looked at him and narrowed my eyes.

"There is *one* thing you've forgotten," he said, and scribbled tentatively at the bottom of the list:

"COULD BE A SUPERVILLAIN??"

I rolled my eyes. Not this again. "Look. No one wants him to be a supervillain more than me, OK?" I said. "But let's be realistic. Just because he drives a rocket car, has a zoo full of pimped-up man-eating animals, a mountain-top retreat and a hollowed-out volcano, it doesn't mean he's some crazed villain who's trying to destroy the world!"

"What about the Global Domination Plan?!" said Viv.

"He was talking about his drinks company!" I retorted. "Look, if you can give me just one bit of evidence that supervillains even *exist*, let alone that Pheel might actually be one, then maybe I'll believe you. Otherwise, I'm calling the shots."

Viv lowered his head and looked miserable. Then, like a street lamp at dusk, he lit up. "I know! Follow me!"

"Come in!" chimed Mr Meringue. He was sitting at his desk in his empty classroom, his little moustache twitching with each cross he planted on a test. Viv strode in confidently and I followed behind. The room smelt of old books and floor polish.

"Viv . . . and Billy! To what do I owe this pleasure?" he asked, taking a sip of tea from his mug.

"*Salve*, Mr Meringue!" said Viv, with a bow.

Mr Meringue allowed himself a smile and replied. "*Salve*, Viv!" It was a geeky Roman joke, I think. "*Sedet, sedet!*" He gestured towards two chairs.

"Mr Meringue, can we ask you a history question?" Viv asked.

"Of course, boys!" he replied. "My door is always *apertus*." He gave a little wink and his moustache bristled with satisfaction. Viv returned a grin. I told you: these guys have a weird history thing going on between them.

"Supervillains exist in real life, don't they?" said Viv, firmly and directly. "You said so the other day."

Mr Meringue was momentarily taken aback, before settling into the question.

"Well, boys, your usual comic-book villains – your 'Jokers', your 'Penguins', your 'Riddlers'." He made little inverted comma signs with his fingers when he said each name. "They are all the stuff of fantasy." I could sense Viv's confidence waver. "But that's because real-life supervillains are much better at hiding in plain sight. Just look at Al Capone. He didn't go around in green face paint or dressed as a flightless bird! But that doesn't mean he wasn't a very, very bad man. A . . ." He used his fingers as quotation marks again. ". . . 'supervillain', if you will. So in answer – yes, they do exist."

He sat back, interlinked his fingers across his patterned tank top and twitched his moustache again.

Viv shuffled forward on his chair. "So if they're not walking around in an eye mask . . ." Mr Meringue allowed himself a little smile at this. ". . . how would we spot them?"

I momentarily let my mind wander, imagining what

Pheel would look like in an eye mask. It'd be purple, probably. And probably made in silk like his suits. I pictured it in my mind and something began to nag at me, but I couldn't put my finger on what.

Mr Meringue cleared his throat and I snapped back into the room. "I suppose that if there was a supervillain at large, they would be incredibly rich and charismatic." He looked up the ceiling and bounced his eyebrows. He was clearly enjoying himself now. "Perhaps they would be flashy with it. And overly generous. They would dress themselves up as a Robin Hood figure. . ."

"In tights with a longbow!" exclaimed Viv, his excitement getting the better of him.

Mr Meringue chuckled. "No, no, no! I mean they would hand out free gifts and money to local people and politicians – build a groundswell of support to mask their more *devious* operations."

I sat up to attention. This was sounding more and more like Pheel.

He continued: "They would have lots of henchmen – crime bosses very rarely do their own dirty work. And there would be no end to their ambitions. All the biggest villains want one thing only – global domination!"

I was speechless. My brain felt like it might burst. Mr Meringue had described Pheel down to his try-hard pants. Now that I heard it like this, I could see it wasn't just a product of Viv's overactive imagination. Every single bit of him completely fit the profile of a supervillain. But there was something even bigger bugging me. I couldn't get the image of him in his purple eye mask out of my head. I pictured him with it wrapped around his head, his try-hard eyes poking out through the holes. Then I pictured him vanishing, leaving the eye mask suspended in mid-air. It hung there for a second then, like a dropped tissue, fluttered to the floor in a crumpled heap, its bow still tied and the little eyeholes glaring upwards... And I suddenly realized what was nagging at me. I knew where I'd seen the crumpled heap of silk before – on Pheel's dashboard! How could I have been so stupid! It wasn't a purple handkerchief he'd left lying around in his rocket car – it was an eye mask!

I looked across at Viv, my jaw practically on the floor. He was hanging on the edge of his seat, more juiced up than if he'd drunk twenty PholaColas. He opened his mouth and the words fell out like fumbled hand grenades. "WE THINK BILLY'S STEPDAD IS A SUPERVILLAIN!" Viv slapped a hand across his mouth but it was too late. Mr Meringue watched each word explode in horror, then began angrily shuffling his papers. "Now boys, I see what this was all about. A trap! A trap for poor Mr Meringue. How foolish of me! Mr Pern, a supervillain? Don't be so silly. He is an incredible ambassador for this town. He is generous, charming and he goes out of the way to help others," he said, his voice bristling with hurt. Then he reached down and took a slurp from his mug. A dribble of liquid ran down his chin and I realized that it wasn't tea in there. It was PholaCola.

"And he makes a most delicious drink. Now – run along, the pair of you, and don't come back with any more silly questions!"

CHAPTER 5
Hacking the Database

"I swear on my life, I didn't imagine it," I said, swinging through Viv's front gate. "Pheel had an eye mask on his dashboard! Just like the Riddler or Catwoman wears."

Viv strode beside me in stunned silence. I could almost hear the cogs in his brain whirring.

"And *everything* about him fits Mr Meringue's profile!" I continued. "I have to admit it ... I think you're right."

Viv was staring wide-eyed into space. I don't think he'd blinked since I told him about the eye mask. He slowly pulled the front-door key out of his pocket, then paused as his eyes darted back and forth in thought.

"Mr Meringue's description and you spotting that eye mask isn't enough. We need real evidence," he muttered, staring vacantly at his front step. Something was hatching in his brain, I could sense it. He sprang back to life and slipped the key into the lock. "I've got an idea."

We stepped inside and dumped our rucksacks by the front door.

"Halt! Who goes there!" came the shout from the kitchen. Viv's dad swung out from behind the door frame. In one hand, he was holding a Snickers bar and pretending it was a gun, while in the other, he gripped his tarnished police badge.

"Hello, Mr Burman," I said, slipping off my shoes and following Viv in.

"Hi there, Billy," he said, panting from exhaustion and taking a bite of his Snickers.

He waddled towards us in his socks and ruffled Viv's hair.

"Where are your trousers?" asked Viv.

"Took them off," he replied, finishing his Snickers and wiping his nose on his sleeve. "My legs got hot after a tough day fighting crime!" he said, triumphantly. "The old man at number thirty-two thought a burglar was hiding in his cupboard. Turns out it was a squirrel."

He waddled back into the kitchen and made a beeline for a pack of doughnuts. By the look of the jam caught in his stubble, this wasn't his first.

"But the poor old squirrel was spooked as hell... Doughnut?" he asked, looking up at me. I nodded. He popped a doughnut each on a plate for me and Viv, then scooped up four for himself. "So we had to shoot it."

Viv was standing by the kitchen dresser with his back to us, looking shifty. But this caught his attention. "You shot a squirrel?!" he spluttered.

Mr Burman stuffed half a doughnut in his mouth. A little jet of jam rolled down his chin. "Just with a Taser. Low-voltage, of course." A chubby tongue poked out from his lips and mopped up the stray jam. "Little chap's in the cells now, cooling off. He'll be fine. I took the rest of the day off because of the stress of it and whatnot."

He licked the sugar from the outside of his doughnut as his attention moved on to the TV, which was blaring in the corner. It was the news. On the screen, a short fat man with a nose like a red golf ball stood behind a lectern. It was the town mayor, Ron Blarblorn. He was wearing plush purple robes and a gold medallion and it looked like he was holding some sort of press conference. Behind him hung a banner with the words: "WHAT ARE YOU DOING?"

"People say I was wrong to cut the police numbers!" boomed Mayor Blarblorn into the camera. "But I had no choice!"

Mr Burman muttered something under his breath that sounded like an insult. Mum had already told me that the mayor had sacked lots of police officers. It boggled my mind to think that Mr Burman still had a job. But I suppose *someone* had to stay; those squirrels weren't going to taser themselves.

"So I'm officially launching our new campaign – 'What are *you* doing?'" Mayor Blarblorn continued, light bulbs flashes bouncing off his shiny round face. "I want to encourage every citizen to step up and help keep this town safe – and not rely on the police to do it all for them!"

Mr Burman turned the TV off and bit into his doughnut angrily.

"Stupid mayor," he muttered.

Behind us, Viv still hovered shiftily at the back of the room. He was up to something, I knew it.

"We're going upstairs to do some homework," he said, crab-stepping towards the kitchen door.

Mr Burman raised a sticky hand in acknowledgement and Viv made a frantic "Come here" sign at me from the hallway, before bounding up the stairs. I thanked Mr Burman for the doughnut and hurried after.

He reached the top of the stairs and lifted his finger to his lips. "Sshhhhhhh," he whispered, then took a sidestep towards his dad's bedroom door, twisted the handle and pushed it open. "Quickly!" he whispered, ushering me in.

I wasn't quite sure what was going on, but I did as I was told.

Viv slipped in after, then silently closed the door and tiptoed over to his dad's computer.

"What are you doing?" I hissed.

He slipped a card from his pocket and held it up to

me. It said "POLICE ACCESS ID" and had a photo of his dad on it. It made sense now: *that's* what he'd been doing by the dresser – stealing his dad's ID card! Viv slid it into a slot on the computer and pressed the space bar. A window flashed up on-screen.

"**INTERNATIONAL CRIMINAL DATABASE**," it said.

I knew *exactly* what Viv was up to. And I also knew just how much trouble we'd both be in if we were caught.

A little box popped up saying: "**PASSWORD**".

We locked eyes. "Drat," I said with a wince. Nice try, but how were we going to hack into a police database...?

Viv thought for a second, then typed in "**PASSWORD**".

"**PASSWORD SUCCESSFUL**," a little box said. The more I thought about it, the more astonishing it was that his dad still had a job.

A search bar appeared on-screen, asking for a name, an address or date of birth.

Viv hurriedly typed in: "**PHIL PERN**". Then he took a nervous breath and whispered, "If your stepdad has ever been arrested or even cautioned by police, this database will tell us!" Then he hit the return key. "This is real, proper *evidence*!"

A buzz of excitement rippled through me as an activity bar worked its way across the screen. Then the computer crunched, hummed and the words "**NO SEARCH RESULTS**" popped up on-screen. I felt myself deflate.

"Try his full name, 'Phileas Pern'," I whispered.

Viv typed it in.

"**NO SEARCH RESULTS.**"

"His home address?" I said.

"**NO SEARCH RESULTS.**"

"His volcano address?"

"**NO SEARCH RESULTS.**"

"What about his date of birth?" I said. "I know he had his birthday on the tenth last month, and he was forty-two . . . so that would mean. . ."

Viv was one step ahead of me, punching the corresponding digits into the search field. The activity bar scrolled and this time it threw up lines and lines of names . . . across dozens of pages. I felt a little pang of hope.

Viv feverishly scanned down the screen. Suddenly, the creak of footsteps sounded from the stairs.

"Quick, your dad's coming!"

In a flash, Viv moved the cursor to the print icon and clicked. The printer made a gargling noise and began spitting out pages. The footsteps were on the landing now . . . the door handle was turning . . . the door opening. . . The printer spat out the last page. . . In a flash, Viv grabbed them, whipped his dad's card from its slot, stuffed them all up his jumper and jammed his finger into the computer's off button.

"Boys! You know this computer's not for games!" Mr Burman was standing in the doorway, panting from climbing the stairs.

We swung around and flashed him our best "guilty but sorry" faces and hurried out as quickly as we could, the evidence rustling reassuringly inside Viv's jumper.

CHAPTER 6
The Secret Cellar

The database pages lay spread out across my bedroom floor and we both stared at them morosely. This must have been the twentieth time we'd read them. About fifteen times yesterday at Viv's house, and another five times today at mine. There were thirty-two sheets in total, and fifty names per sheet. That made sixteen hundred names, by Viv's count. And every single one of them had a pencil line through it. The air stank of disappointment. And also slightly of burp.

"We've got to have missed one! We need to go through them again!" said Viv, scrunching up a finished

can of PholaCola, getting down on all fours and scanning the pages.

I sighed. "Face it, buddy: Pheel's not on there."

Viv pushed his face even closer to the sheets. "Come on! I was *sure* this was going to work!"

I had to put it to Viv: when he set his mind on something, he wouldn't let it go. But the database had spelt it out loud and clear: Pheel had never had any sort of brush with the law. Ever. Not in this town. Not in this country. Not on this planet. He was squeaky clean. And supervillains were *never* squeaky clean.

I pulled myself from my bed and began gathering the sheets together. "Let it go, buddy. Maybe we need to take a step back. It could just be coincidence that he matches Mr Meringue's description. And he could've had that eye mask for any number of reasons: masquerade ball . . . fancy dress ball . . . some other type of ball. . ."

Then why did he snatch it up so guiltily? my brain yelled at me, but I did my best to ignore it.

"You said it yourself – we need proper evidence. And we haven't got *any*. I need a realistic way to break up Mum and Pheel. And telling her that he is a supervillain – without any evidence to back it up – isn't going to cut it."

Viv was refusing to give up. "I *know* that uncovering this is the best way to break up your mum and Pheel. I just *know* it!"

You had to give Viv full marks for commitment – he really wanted to find a way of keeping me in Blemish. I rolled the papers up and slipped them in my back pocket. "Come on, let's get you another PholaCola to calm you down." I was worried that if I didn't snap him out of his obsession he'd grow old in this room: poring over the sheets, his long white beard all matted and smelly, whispering "Phileas Pern" over and over again in the moonlight, while I lived a million miles away in the Alps.

He reluctantly rose to his feet, shaking his head in exasperation. I opened my bedroom door into the soulless white corridor that snaked for miles and miles around the Obserphatory.

"I appreciate the effort, I really do," I said, as our trainers squeaked along the shiny floor. "But maybe we should try a different angle to break them up?"

"No! I'm certain! If we keep looking, I know we'll find proper evidence! I know it." The guy was gabbling now. He was in too deep.

A manservant silently whizzed past us in an electric golf buggy as I pressed the button for the elevator. It pinged and the shiny metal doors slid open. We stepped inside and I could see Viv's face still creased with injustice, like the truth was right in front of our noses but we weren't seeing it.

"We should follow that manservant – try and question him!" he said.

I looked Viv up and down. He hardly fit the profile of your usual grizzled interrogator. I let him down, gently: "You know they never say anything."

"Or we should tap Pheel's phone!"

"And exactly how are you going to do that?"

Viv's desperation reached fever pitch. "Come on! I'm not wrong! I know in my gut that I'm not wrong! We're just not using our eyes!" He spun around, searching the elevator, as if he might fight a dossier of supervillainry in the six-foot-by-six-foot box. "Like this – this 'C' here!" He was gesticulating wildly at the elevator controls. "It could stand for cave! As in *bat cave*! Or chamber! As in *torture chamber*! Or c—"

"I think it stands for cellar," I interrupted. "As in *wine cellar*."

"But how do you know?" he asked. "HOW DO YOU KNOW?"

"Fine," I said, and pushed the "C" button. "If you really wanna check, let's check."

The elevator dropped. *4 – 3 – 2...* Viv hopped anxiously from foot to foot. *1 – G – C. Ping!* The doors slid open to reveal...

"Oh..." said Viv, his chin sinking to his chest.

In front of us lay a dark, dank wine cellar. A single bare light bulb illuminated the metal wine racks, and a smell of mould fogged the air.

I looked at him, my lips pursed in sympathy.

Viv blinked disbelievingly and staggered from the shiny metal elevator into the dingy cellar and mumbled: "I was so sure..."

I stared around the dank brick room. I'd never been down here before. But then again, why would I have? I wandered aimlessly from the lift and inspected the rows of wine bottles lining the walls, blowing off the layers of dust to reveal old, peeling labels.

Something bright caught my eye in a wine rack near the floor. It looked like a purple PholaCola label. I crouched down and examined it in its slot. It was full and the lid was still sealed. *This should cheer Viv up!* I thought, and reached down to grab it. But it was stuck. *How weird.* I pulled and wiggled it but it wouldn't come free. I tried twisting it and it spun around easily with a *click click click*. But it *still* wouldn't come free. I spun it back. *Click click click.* Suddenly, an ear-splitting groan filled the room and the floor began to shake like there was an earthquake.

"Whooooaaa! What's going on?" cried Viv, his legs wobbling like a new-born lamb.

"I don't know!" I cried, flapping my arms to keep balance.

The coarse sound of rock grating against rock filled my brain and I realized that the floor wasn't shaking; it was moving! In fact: it was spinning!

My legs collapsed and I fell to my knees as the floor spun and spun and then, with an abrupt jerk, stopped.

"Whoa!" I said, feeling dizzy and sick as I pushed myself up from all fours.

"OH MY GOODNESS GRAPES!" said Viv, accidentally making up a brand-new exclamation. "B-b-bat c-c-c-cave!"

I looked up and my mouth fell open. We weren't in the wine cellar any more, we were in a. . .

"Bat . . . cave," I stammered.

I must have activated some sort of secret revolving door because the dingy cellar was gone, and in its place was a secret, state-of-the-art lair. Everything was bright and white and squeaky clean. In front of us, a giant curved screen stretched along the wall, with an enormous control panel just below it. On one side of the room, a dozen of Pheel's purple suits hung in perfect unison. And on the other sat a cabinet of exotic weapons – a crossbow, a sabre, a flamethrower – all individually lit like museum exhibits. It certainly wasn't your average home office.

"B-b-b-bat c-c-c-cave," stuttered Viv again.

"Let's not jump to conclusions. . ." I muttered. But inside, my brain was screaming: **BAT CAVE!**

My tummy was swirling, half in excitement, half in trepidation.

I edged gingerly towards the suits and picked one from the rail. "Perhaps this is just his walk-in wardrobe?" I offered, meekly. ". . .In a secret den hidden behind a wine rack. . ." Just saying it out loud made it sound ridiculous.

As I lifted the suit, a purple silk cloth fluttered from the hanger and crumpled on the shiny white floor. My heart skipped a beat. I didn't need to pick it up to know what it was, but I did anyway. In my hand sat a purple, silk eye mask.

"What is it? What is it?" said Viv.

I held it up to him. His eyes became the size of Wagon Wheels and he mumbled: "Goodness grapes. . . It's his supervillain outfit. . ."

I looked from the eye mask to the suit. Now I was inspecting it closely, I could see that it wasn't your usual suit. There were trousers – nothing odd about that. A jacket – all fine there. And . . . a glossy collared cape, embroidered with the letters "Mr P". *What???*

I scanned the rail. Every single suit was the same. My

brain felt swamped with the magnitude of what we'd just found. Viv had been right all along. This changed EVERYTHING.

"We've f-f-f-found his supervillain lair!" said Viv, his face a mix of glee and terror. He stepped towards the control panel and, with a shaky hand, dared to press a button on the keyboard.

The giant screen flickered and sprang alive, casting an eerie reflective light across the white surfaces.

"Holy macaroni," I spluttered.

"Goodness grapes..." muttered Viv.

Plastered across the giant screen was a presentation with the words: "GLOBAL DOMINATION PLAN".

Then below it, in smaller fonts, it said: "Agenda for PH meeting on 17 May. Chaired by Mr Pernicious."

Both our mouths hung wide open.

Viv mumbled out loud: "Phil Pern... Mr Pernicious... That must be his supervillain name!"

"Press it again! Press it again!" I said. Whether Pheel was planning an aggressive international drinks promotion, or plotting to destroy the world, this presentation was about to tell us. Viv lifted a shaky finger. My heart was beating like an octopus on a drum kit. Pheel could walk in any second. Viv pressed the arrow key. A memory stick slotted in the front of the computer blinked, and the screen scrolled to page two.

"Item #1: vote on new name," said the presentation.

"OK ... nothing incriminating there ..." I said. "Next page."

Viv scrolled on.

"Item #2: discussion re stationery," said the presentation.

"OK ... this isn't looking *that* damning," I muttered, with a flicker of frustration.

Viv clicked on to the next page and our jaws hit the floor.

"Item #3: current plans for global revenge on humanity."

Viv looked at me with a mixture of intense vindication and absolute horror. The blood drained from his face and his eyes were strained, but he had forced a smile. "See. I knew I was right," he croaked.

Viv's hand was shaking so much he could hardly hit

the arrow key. He just about managed to press it, but the page didn't change.

"T-t-t-that's it," he stammered.

My whole insides were now whizzing, including my brain. Viv *had* been right all along . . . Pheel WAS a supervillain. And he WAS plotting against humanity! This was terrible! Diabolical! And Mum would absolutely HATE it!

"Grab that USB stick!" I whisper-shouted, my pulse pounding in my ears. "We need this as evidence."

"Which USB stick?" Viv was pale, panicky.

"That one!" I said, pointing at the front of the computer.

Viv reached a trembling hand out and yanked the USB stick from its socket.

"What are you doing!" I hissed. "You've got to eject it first! Everyone knows you have to eject a USB first!"

Viv was flustered. "What? How? Do they?"

A window popped up on the giant screen: "MEMORY STICK EJECTED PREMATURELY. DISC CORRUPTED."

"Arggghhhh!" I hit my palm against my forehead. I

wanted to get out of there that second, and I sensed Viv did as well. If Pheel walked in. . . Well, goodness knows what a supervillain does to spies.

"We've no time. We'll fix it later. Come on!"

I grabbed Viv and dragged him back to the wine rack, then frantically twisted the PholaCola bottle trigger. The screech of stone on stone filled the room and the wall swung 180 degrees, spitting us back out in the wine cellar. We stood there for a moment, dizzy, panting, trying to absorb what had just happened.

"He's plotting a global revenge. . ." mumbled Viv. He was trembling like a jelly on a washing machine.

"Come on!" I pulled him into the lift and punched the "4" button for my bedroom. The metal doors slid shut and the elevator shot upwards. Viv was drenched in sweat. I was tingling with a mix of terror and excitement. We needed to get back to my bedroom and hide the USB stick ASAP! Who knows what other incriminating stuff was on it?! If we could get it working, it would give us the evidence we needed to break Mum and Pheel up. In fact, even better – it might be enough evidence to get Pheel locked up in prison!

The elevator slowed, then pulled to a halt. "SECOND FLOOR," said the automatic voice.

"What?"

"DOORS OPENING."

No! I punched the "4" button again and again, but it was no use. The doors slid open and there, on the other side, stood Phil.

I froze as he glowered at us, his eyes cold as bullets. I gulped and Viv whimpered. Then he sprang his fake smile on us and stepped in.

"What are you boys up to?" he asked, pressing a button as the doors closed.

The words fell out of my mouth in a blabbering stream: "Nothing. Absolutely nothing. Nothing. Why do you ask? We haven't been doing anything. Nothing."

Viv echoed, in a near silent squeak: "Nothing."

I stuffed my hand in my pocket and wrapped my fist around the USB. It felt like it had a pulse that was thumping against my palm.

He shrugged and let out a forced chuckle. "Just asking, boys." Then he cleared his throat and gave me that awkward look like when he wants to say something but doesn't know how. "I've been, um, thinking. Why don't we have a boys' night in on Saturday? I've got something I'd like to. . ." His fake smile couldn't hide his sense of discomfort. ". . . talk to you about. We'll kick back with a movie and order in some pizza? What's that one you like? Pizza House?"

"OK. Sure. Thanks," replied a tense Viv. I don't think the invite was meant for him but I was glad he'd completely misread the situation; I'd much prefer to have him there as a buffer to Pheel.

Pheel looked even more uncomfortable and opened his mouth to retract the invite, but I got in there first: "Sure, we'd both love to come."

"FOURTH FLOOR," announced the elevator.

I grabbed Viv and pulled him out of the lift after me. "Gotta go, now. Bye!" The doors slid shut before Pheel could get another word in. I stood there in the hallway, Viv white as a sheet next to me, feeling like my heart was about to explode.

Finally, I croaked: "Let's take a look at this USB, then."

*

Viv and I perched on my bed with my laptop. I inserted the USB into the computer and prayed. It made a cranking noise and the message sprang up:

"**USB DRIVE CORRUPTED**."

"*Farts!*" I shouted, slapping my hand angrily against my keyboard. "We were so close! Who knows how much more incriminating evidence there is on there! What are we going to do now?"

Viv took a breath and composed himself. He was still pretty shaky from the Pheel run-in. "I was thinking. . . There *is* one place we could take it. . ."

I looked up at him cautiously. And then it hit me. I knew exactly where he meant, and he was right. But it would be the riskiest move of our lives.

CHAPTER 7
This Must Be IT

I shovelled my cornflakes into my mouth at lightning speed. I desperately wanted to wolf them down and get out of the Obserphatory before Pheel turned up for breakfast. I felt on edge with the USB stick in my pocket. And if I could avoid him, it'd be two hundred times easier.

"You're quiet today, sweetie," said Mum from across the table.

I shrugged and pulled an "Am I?" face, then continued cramming cornflakes into my gob.

She looked down at her newspaper, then seemed to remember something. "I hear you and Phil are having a boys' night in on Saturday?"

71

"And Viv!" I sprayed.

She smiled. "Thank you, sweetie. For spending time with Phil. It means a lot to me."

I could sense what this was all about. It was as obvious as a fart in a Zorb ball – Pheel had been told to have a "chat" with me. Try and smooth things over after the whole *loser* thing. Well, if I played my cards right, he'd be locked up in jail by the time Saturday arrived.

I sprang up and stuck my empty bowl in the sink.

"Gotta go." I planted a kiss on Mum's cheek. "I'm, erm, going to Viv's before school."

The kitchen door swung open and I scrunched my face up in frustration. Pheel strolled into the kitchen stroking his ginger beard and looking vexed.

"Morning," he said, sounding uncharacteristically subdued.

"Morning, darling," said Mum.

"Morning," I muttered under my breath. I reached for the door handle, but something about his behaviour made me hesitate.

"Everything OK?" asked Mum.

"Yes... Yes..." he said distantly, pulling up a chair

at the kitchen table and staring out the window in thought. Then he turned to look from Mum to me, worry creases ploughed across his forehead. "Neither of you has been . . . anywhere unusual in the house, have you?"

My blood turned cold. "Nope. Uh-uh," I said, shaking my head furiously.

"Whereabouts do you mean?" asked Mum.

"Oh, nowhere. Just thinking out loud," he said, shrugging and snapping to. "Pass the cornflakes, please."

He reached out a hand and his purple suit jacket fell open slightly. That's when I saw it, rolled up and tucked in his inside pocket – the police database list! It must have fallen out of my pocket in the cellar! My insides turned to jelly. He knew someone was on to him! I HAD to get out of there before he spotted my guilty face.

"Bye!" I spluttered, grabbing my bike helmet and bundling out the kitchen door in a state of half panic. We'd made our first mistake. And I just prayed that we could get the evidence off this USB stick to bring down

Pheel before he worked out that it was missing . . . and that it was us who had stolen it!

I hovered anxiously by a door in the school hallway, waiting for Viv. It had been a long, long day of lessons. And now, Viv and I were about to embark on one of the riskiest missions of our lives – or our social lives, at least. On the other side of that door was . . . IT Club.

OK, I know what you're thinking – getting a bunch of nerds to fix your USB stick doesn't sound particularly dangerous. But when you are Viv and me, dicing with IT Club was pretty much social suicide. They were the only people who kept us off rock bottom on the popularity ladder; the only people we could divert attention on to when the bullies targeted us.

Someone does a fart in class? Everyone blames Billy or Viv. So what do we do? Blame one of IT Club. Brayden Balls wants to steal our lunch. What do we do? Tell him that Darius from IT Club is packing three bags of premium crisps and a king-sized Kit Kat in his lunch box. It was a tried-and-tested formula. And it's all that kept school life bearable. So, if Brayden Balls and his pals saw us hanging out with IT, they'd think we were one of them. The tried-and-tested formula would be useless. We'd be writing our own social death warrants.

I scanned the hallway anxiously and hopped from foot to foot.

"Hi. I'm here. Sorry," said Viv, bursting around a corner, panting.

I cracked open the IT Club door, pushed him through and bundled in after. The air was hot and sticky, and smelt like boiled sweets and BO.

A long, slow nasal snort sounded from across the room. "Billy Benbow and Viv Burman? I wondered when you were finally going to join us." It was Darius Bernard (pronounced the French way, even though he was as English as a pork pie). He was swinging nonchalantly on his office chair, his face a tapestry of acne and bumfluff. His IT Club cronies all laughed through their nostrils.

"We're not here to join you," I replied. "We just need your help."

Darius turned smugly to his cronies. "So! Billy Benbow wants our help!"

They snorted some more. He was probably still

smarting from the time Brayden Balls accused me of having three nipples so I told everyone that Darius had four bumholes. I realized now that, after years of this kind of thing, I had zero bargaining power.

Viv blurted out. "It's a matter of international importance!"

"Ooooo!" said Darius, sarcastically. "What is it, want us to design a bin-proof head for you, Billy Bin Boy?"

Cue more nostril laughter. Being taunted by IT Club. This was a new low. I had no choice but to suck it up. If I wanted their help busting Pheel, I was going to have to get creative.

"Viv's right. Whatever is on this USB stick is of international importance. And whoever can help us decrypt it is going to get a LOT of credit. Newspaper headlines. Rolling news coverage." I took a deep breath and glanced at the poster of a supermodel pinned to the wall. "Loads of attention from famous girls. . . But I guess you're not interested."

I spun around and reached for the door.

Viv hissed in my ear: "We can't leave. They are our last hope."

"Trust me!" I hissed back, and prayed my reverse psychology would pay off.

Someone was whispering behind me: "Darius – if he's right, this could fast-track Project Supermodel!"

Darius let a nasal huff of annoyance. I turned the handle and cracked the door. . .

"All right, OK, let's take a look," he said.

Bingo! I let the door click shut.

"Bring it over here!" he huffed, swinging around to face his computer.

I wove through the half dozen club members to Darius's desk and handed over the USB stick. The deeper I went into the room, the hotter it became. A boy with a blond bowl cut offered me a boiled egg from his lunch box. I declined.

Darius plugged in the USB stick and began furiously punching keys. Streams of black-and-white data flew up the computer screen.

Viv smiled politely at the boiled-egg boy and asked, "What's Project Supermodel?"

Darius held a hand up to stop his crony answering, then pointed towards the poster. It was of a short, not-very-attractive tech millionaire standing next to a very beautiful woman.

"You think he was able to date a supermodel because of his looks? Or his personality?" snorted Darius, his bumfluff moustache bristling at the suggestion. "Of course not! He did it because he made millions from coding!"

I nodded. Made sense.

Darius continued: "What chance do you think poor Frank has of bagging a beautiful girlfriend?" He gestured towards boiled-egg boy, who offered a meek wave in reply. "None! But once he can earn millions coding, he'll be able to date thousands of girls!"

Darius attacked his keyboard with fresh venom, scanning new lines of data as they flew by. "Project Supermodel is what we are all in it for. Earn millions. Woo supermodels. Rule the world! Inside these four walls, we might be geeks. But out there. . ." He trailed off.

Out there, I thought. We'd all like to be someone different *out there.* But you had to be realistic.

Viv looked momentarily enticed by the project, until

Frank bit into his boiled egg. "We're all going to go out with supermodels!" he said, spraying old grey yolk crumbs across his lap.

I forced a smile. "Sure you are, Frank. Sure you are," I replied. The temptation drained from Viv's eyes.

Darius pulled the USB stick from its socket and spun around to face Viv and me. "What you've got here is a real doozy of a memory stick," he said, holding it in front of him. "Yes, it's slightly damaged because someone didn't eject it properly. . ."

Viv coughed and looked at his feet.

"However, that wouldn't be hard to fix. But, underneath it, you have three levels of sophisticated encryption. The kind of encryption you'd need a superhacker to crack."

There was a brief silence, before Viv asked: "Are *you* a superhacker?"

Darius laughed coldly at the suggestion. "I am not. Neither is Frank here, nor Andy, Craig, Samantha, Mo or Bert."

IT Club shook its head in unison.

I felt the hope drain out of me.

"However, there is . . . *someone* who could help," said Darius, then lowered his voice. "Consignia."

IT Club broke into shocked whispers: "Consignia?"

Darius silenced them by raising his hand, then cleared his throat. "There's a legend of a superhacker who attended this school not so long ago. Who they are, where they live, what they look like – no one knows. All we know is that, if we want to get hold of them, we can leave a message on a special page deep inside the Dark Web. If they accept the job, they will get in touch with you directly."

"And if they don't accept the job?" asked Viv.

Darius shook his head. "You will hear nothing."

"Can you do it? Can you post?" I was practically begging.

Darius nodded. "Yes. But I warn you – they have never replied to any of our requests yet. Not when Katie Smithers erased her school project. Not even when we couldn't get past level fourteen of Questland."

"Make sure you say it is of international importance!" said Viv. "The future of the world depends on it!"

Darius looked him up and down suspiciously, then shrugged. "OK." And turned back to his computer.

"Thanks, Darius," I said. His back still turned to us, he lifted a limp hand in acknowledgement. Fizzing with new hope, we turned to leave.

"Erm ... Billy?" said Darius. I turned over my shoulder.

"Yeah?"

His voice had an uncharacteristic fragility. "When this all sorts itself out, you will give us a credit, right? Put a good word in for us with the girls?"

I nodded. "Sure I will, Darius. Sure I will."

Then we slipped out and I closed the door on their pigeonhole, breathing fresh, cool air into my lungs. "We still have hope of getting evidence off this USB, busting Pheel and breaking him up with Mum," I said.

But before Viv could reply, the world went dark.

Brayden Ball's tinny voice exploded through the darkness. "HAHAHAHA! BILLY BIN BOY!"

CHAPTER 8

A Message from the Blue

I sat on Viv's bed with a bin stuck on my head. I was trying to distract myself from the stench by explaining to Viv what had happened at breakfast. With all the dramas of IT Club, I'd forgotten to tell him about it.

"Pheel had the police database list inside his suit pocket – we'd left it in the cellar!"

Viv was behind me, trying to heave the bin off my head. "Ow!" I cried, the plastic grinding against my ears. But the bin didn't budge. "Did you hear me? We left the police database in the cellar."

"Sorry," said Viv. "It's just your voice sounds completely different when your head is in the bin. Say it again."

It had been about two hours since Brayden Balls bin-boy-ed me with an extra-small bin. And this time, it had got wedged on my head – much to his delight. Viv had to lead me back to his house like he was a guide dog. I could hear the sniggers of passing schoolkids from inside my plastic head-prison.

"PHEEL FOUND THE POLICE DATABASE SHEETS!" I shouted. "WE LEFT THEM IN THE CELLAR!"

He looked the bin up and down again. "Maybe we should try soap. . ." He wasn't listening. "You'll have to

put your head upside down, let the soap slide into the bin," he said. I lay on my back and let my head hang off the bed. He poured detergent into the bin and it oozed past my ears. To think – getting bullied by Brayden Balls used to be the sum total of my problems. Now it was just an annoying inconvenience compared to having an evil supervillain stepdad who wanted to wreak his revenge on the world and move to the Alps.

"OK, stand up again."

I moved myself upright. Viv clamped his hands around the bin and heaved. With a pop and a woosh it flew off my head, slipping out of Viv's soapy hands and flying across the room.

"Phew," I said, massaging my neck in relief.

"What was it you were saying?" he asked.

I repeated myself about the database sheets and watched Viv's anxiety skyrocket. "W-w-w-what happens if he finds out it was us?"

I shrugged. "I dunno. I mean, he IS a supervillain. Maybe he'd feed us to his platinum-teethed crocodiles," I half joked.

Viv's face turned white. "We need to get this

evidence off the USB before he works it out. . ." He took a deep breath to try and calm himself. "How long's that going to take. . .? You heard what Darius said, we might never hear from this. . ."

As he was saying it, my phone beeped. A bolt of excitement ran up my spine as I read it. I held it up so Viv could see.

97 MERLIN GROVE
THURSDAY 4 P.M.
CONSIGNIA

"Yes!" He jumped up and punched the air.
The phone bleeped again.

"PS DESTROY THIS MESSAGE. TELL NO ONE. OR YOUR PHONE WILL SELF-DESTRUCT."

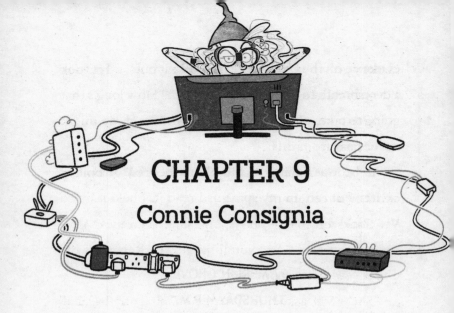

CHAPTER 9
Connie Consignia

"Ninety-seven Merlin Grove. This is it," I said, opening the gate. A pristine front garden gave way to a white bungalow beyond. "Come on," I said, and set off down the cobbled path. Sun-faded garden gnomes smiled up at me from the lawn.

Viv followed nervously, his baseball cap pulled almost over his eyes. He'd got panicky about this Consignia person, and was determined to keep a low profile.

I stepped on to the porch and pressed the doorbell. A shrill buzz sounded inside. Viv shuffled nervously as footsteps approached. Even I was a little anxious.

"Well, hello there!" We were greeted by a short,

chubby grown-up with ruddy cheeks and round glasses. He resembled a giant gnome himself.

"Consignia?" I asked.

"Certainly!" he chimed. "Come on in!"

He stood aside and ushered us in. The bungalow smelt of lavender and bleach.

"Shoes off, please, boys," he said, then eyed Viv's head and tutted. "And you'll have to take that hat off. She is very strict about hats."

"She?" Viv asked, reluctantly slipping the baseball cap from his head. "You're not Consignia?"

He tutted and shook his head. "No, no, no. Connie's downstairs. Follow me."

He led us back into the beige hallway and halted by a door under the stairs.

"I'm so glad she's got some friends visiting. She doesn't get out much," he said, then scratched his head and added: "Ever, in fact."

He pulled open the door. A set of steps vanished into a dim basement. "Down you go, boys."

Viv gulped. I took a deep breath, ducked and stepped through.

"And . . . boys?"

I looked back up the stairs one last time. "Yes?"

"Try and ask her to come upstairs for tea. Just for once."

And with that he closed the door, plunging us into a dingy twilight.

I descended the stairs one at a time. Slow creaks behind told me that Viv was following.

"Hello?" I called. Silence.

There was a hum of computers, and a bluish light shone from the furthest reaches of the dusty basement. I was more nervous than I had been at the front door.

"Hello?" I called again. The static air made my hair tingle.

A girl's voice finally cut through the twilight. "You're not wearing any hats, are you?"

I looked up at Viv, who was clutching his cap in his hands. "Erm, no, I took it off."

"Good," came the reply. "Leave it on the stairs."

He bent down gingerly and placed it on a step. I squinted into the darkness. The computer screens silhouetted the figure of a girl, her back turned to us.

My nerves eased a little. I could see she was perhaps a year or two older than us. She had a shock of frizzy red hair and wore a brown boilersuit.

"What's wrong with hats?" I asked.

She scoffed. "Don't tell me you trust *hats*?"

"Why wouldn't I?" I asked, eyeing Viv's cap suspiciously.

"Er, d'eurgh!" she said. "Hats obviously just exist to let the government read your minds. They bug all hats to keep track of what we're thinking. Tell me, when did you ever *really* need to wear a hat, huh?"

Viv frowned and opened his mouth to answer, but I shook my head to tell him it wasn't worth arguing.

We reached the bottom of the stairs and she gave a final punch of the keyboard, then swung around. Her pale skin – dotted with a patchwork of freckles – glowed in the half-light beneath a pair of those old-fashioned aviator goggles, just like the bloke who drives Chitty Chitty Bang Bang wears.

She eyed us up and down and shrugged. "All right. OK. I mean, I was expecting someone a bit different."

"Different how?" asked Viv, looking at his arms and legs.

"Well – Darius did say that this was a matter of international importance," she replied. "And, you know, you don't look that *internationally important.*"

Viv scrunched his face tighter. "We are!" Then he thought for a nanosecond. "Well, actually, we're not. But what we have on this USB stick is really, really important! Just wait and. . ."

She held her palms up towards us. "Whoa there, aggy pants! Don't get so stressy!"

Viv folded his arms and looked offended.

"I ain't judging you," she continued. "I just said you looked different from what I was *expecting*. You know, you don't look like your typical have-a-go heroes."

"We're not trying to be heroes," I replied. "We're just trying to get my mum to dump my jerk stepdad."

She rolled her eyes and looked away. "No one *tries* to be a hero, dummy. They just do the right thing at the right time, even if it's really, really, really, really hard."

She let the sentence hang in the air. "Erm . . . OK," I replied, and fished the USB stick from my pocket. "So Darius says you can hack this?"

She looked up to the ceiling suspiciously and jumped

off her seat. "Hang on! Don't say a word more until I say so!" She hurried into one of the basement's dark corners and reappeared with two tinfoil cones. "You'll need these. Stop the government reading your minds with their satellites." She reached up, placed them on our heads, then stood back and admired us. "Very fetching!"

I lifted the USB stick again. "So can you. . ."

"D'oh," she interrupted, hitting her palm against her forehead. "I need one myself!"

She darted into the corner again. Viv nudged me with his elbow and said, slightly too loudly: "Billy, I think she's mad!"

She reappeared wearing a tinfoil hat and giving Viv daggers. She'd clearly heard. Viv went red and looked at his shoes.

"Now!" she said, flashing Viv one more dirty look, then turning to me and grinning. "Let's see how I can help."

I went to hand her the stick. She plonked down in her chair and motioned to her desk. "Don't give it to me, dummy. Hand it to the robot."

A little robotic arm extended from under her desk. It

opened and closed its fleshy plastic palm in a "gimme" motion. I tentatively handed it the USB stick.

"I built that," she said, grinning. The robot arm slotted the USB into its drive, then she swung back to her screen and adjusted her glasses. I couldn't work out whether she was full-on mad or just very, very eccentric.

"Help yourself to an aniseed ball," she said, gesturing towards a white paper bag full of marble-sized maroon sweets. I put it in my mouth and gagged at the caustic liquorice.

She popped one in her own mouth. Her full attention was on the lines of code that now scrolled down the screen. The only sound was her knocking the aniseed ball against her teeth.

Finally, she said: "So you go to Blemish School?"

"Yup," I replied. "Darius said you used to go there?"

"Used to," she replied. "Dropped out when Dad permanently grounded me. Doesn't let me out of this basement now. So I homeschool."

I looked around at what was presumably her "home school". It was miserable: low-ceilinged and dingy, with rusty metal cabinets lining the walls.

"Why did your dad ground you?" I asked.

She shrugged. "Who knows why parents do anything?" Then she added, almost as an afterthought: "Oh, and I was expelled for hacking the bursary and embezzling ten thousand pounds." She looked up at me and gave me another maniacal grin. I was leaning towards mad rather than eccentric.

More code flew up the screen. She pushed her glasses up her nose and leaned into her computer eagerly. A loud crack from inside her mouth was either the aniseed ball or a tooth shattering. "Holy macaroni. Why would anyone encrypt a USB stick this much? This is, like, government-level encryption."

Viv sidled up beside me. "Can you crack it?"

"Er, of course!" she retorted, giving him another dirty look. The pair had set out on the wrong foot. "If anyone can, Connie can," she said, pushing up her sleeves and rolling her shoulders. Then she began typing furiously.

Finally, she smacked the keyboard and, as the printer began to spit out pages, she shouted triumphantly: "Yes!" Then in almost the same breath, she cried: "No!" And put her hands on her head.

"What is it?" I asked.

The last of the code disappeared off the top of the screen and she swung around to us with her lips pursed.

"What do you want first?" she asked. "The good news or the bad news?"

"Erm, good news. . .?" I replied.

She popped another aniseed ball into her mouth. "Well, I got into your USB stick. It had about five layers of sophisticated encryption. I managed to print off one file." She whipped a page from the printer and handed it to me. I read it out loud:

"PH Meeting re Global Revenge Plan
17 May
Lord Krung – Hawaii
The Professor – Fiorentina
Madame Mink – Vesuvius."

Viv stared at it and blinked. "Was does it mean?"

I shook my head slowly. "I've got no idea."

"Hawaii, Fiorentina, Vesuvius. Those are all places," said Connie, chirpily.

I looked at her, deadpan. "Thanks."

Then her eyes narrowed and she looked at me suspiciously. "Say ... what's all this about global revenge?"

I looked at her, twinkling in her tinfoil hat. What did it matter if I told someone who never left her basement? Before I knew it, I'd said:

"It's my stepdad. We think he's a ..."

Viv nudged me in the ribs and hissed: "Don't tell her..."

Too late. "... supervillain," I said.

Her eyes grew to the size of pizzas. "AWESOME!" she replied. "Is that what all the other stuff on the drive is about as well?"

My heart gave little flutter of hope. "Other stuff? What other stuff?"

"I'm not completely sure, but it looked like plans, maps, photos, that sort of thing."

"This is exactly what we've been after! Hard evidence!" I cried. "Can we see?"

She screwed her face up. "I said *looked* like. That's the bad news. I'm afraid the USB had some sort of self-destruct code buried deep within it. It gave me about five seconds to print off that page and then. . ." She joined two closed hands together, then expanded them outwards. "KABOOM."

My heart sank.

"Kaboom?" asked Viv, incredulously.

She nodded. "Kaboom. Classic self-destruction code. It was super-smart stuff, you know. No other hacker in the world would have got around it."

My stomach knotted. We were so close to getting a mother lode of dirt on Pheel's evil plans. Surely, it'd have been enough to get Mum to dump him. Instead, all we had was a page of words we didn't understand. I folded it up and stuffed it into my pocket. Connie sat on her hands and leaned forward.

"Do you need help? You know – with taking on your stepdad?" My gaze moved slowly from her tinfoil hat to Viv. He widened his eyes and subtly shook his head.

I forced a smile. "Erm. We'll let you know."

Her excitement ratcheted up a notch. "Cool! I mean, Dad won't let me out of this basement, not even for mealtime . . ." I thought of the mild-mannered man who had let us in and asked us to coax her upstairs for dinner. Something didn't ring true there. "He says I'm too much for the world. Too dangerous. But I can help from down here! You know, with research and hacking and stuff!"

"Um, er. . ." I looked at the stairs. She was friendly and all, but she was crazier than a glittered hyena. And I could tell that Viv didn't like her. He liked people who were safe and predictable – like Mr Meringue – and she was about as safe and predictable as a jack-in-the-box full of a dog poo. "Sure. Probably. Maybe," I said.

"Well! You know where to find me!" she said, puffing out her chest.

"Down here?" said Viv, sarcastically.

"You got it, Sourface!" she replied.

Viv opened his mouth to come back at her, but I grabbed his arm and steered him towards the stairs. "OK. Thanks, Consignia," I said, then lied through my teeth. "I'm sure we'll see you soon!"

She grinned and gave me a little salute, her robot hand waving goodbye beside her. "Brilliant! Call me any time!" she said, then added: "And call me Connie!"

CHAPTER 10
The Bat Cave Revisited

I sat on my bed, staring at the sheet of paper Connie had printed. Every time I looked at it my stomach twisted in frustration: here I was with an evil supervillain for a stepdad, and the only thing I had to prove it was an incomprehensible sheet of paper.

Maybe, though, I might never need to decipher it. There was *one* other piece of evidence that would show Mum what Pheel was really like: the Bat Cave. If Mum could see the weapons and the costumes, and the fact that Pheel was keeping it all a secret from her, she'd be bound to dump him. I didn't have much time to waste before Plan Alps happened, so I had to act.

I found Mum vacuuming the floor of the Obserphatory dome. I strode over and tapped her on the shoulder. She looked up, smiled and switched off the vacuum.

"Hello, sweetie," she said. "So many leaves get blown in here when Phil has the roof open."

Above our heads, the domed Obserphatory roof was split open like a crocus – its four quarters peeled apart to let the early summer sunshine pour in. "There's some or other big thing arriving by helicopter in the next few days," she said, winding the vacuum cord in. "Something to do with the new PholaCola flavour."

I nodded without really listening, then glanced around for any henchmen. The coast was clear. I fidgeted anxiously as I said: "Mum? There's, erm, something I need to show you."

She sensed the seriousness in my voice. "Are you OK?"

"Yeah. It's not me... It's Pheel. Come with me," I said, giving her a little tug on her sleeve.

I set off towards the elevator, pulling her after. "Billy, you're worrying me," she said. "Won't you tell me what's going on?"

"No. I need to show you," I replied, repeatedly punching the elevator button.

PING!

The doors slid open and I pulled her inside. I pressed the "C" button and the elevator began to drop.

"Pheel's got secrets, Mum," I said.

"His name is Phil," she replied, her voice taking on a brittle edge. "And I'm sure we all have our little secrets."

"No! Big secrets! I need to show you."

We ground to a halt and the doors slid open, revealing the dank cellar.

"Come on," I said. She followed begrudgingly.

I scanned the wine racks and clocked the bottle of PholaCola.

"Pheel isn't who he says he is," I said. "He's a villain."

I could sense Mum's body tense. She folded her arms.

"And not just any villain. A supervillain!"

She turned to leave. "Billy. I haven't got time for. . ."

I pulled her back, then crouched down beside the PholaCola bottle. I could hear her tapping a foot impatiently. "Just look at this!" I said, and took a breath to steady my nerves. I spun the bottle around. It felt different from before. It was easier to turn and it wasn't making a clicking noise. "What the. . .?" I muttered.

I could feel Mum's eyes boring into the back of my head.

I spun it back. Still no clicking. I gave it a yank and it slid from the rack with ease. I let out a panicked whimper. "That wasn't supposed to happen. It's supposed to trigger an entrance to Pheel's secret lair!"

Mum's body language radiated fury. I frantically fumbled around the other wine bottles, desperately spinning them and pulling them from the rack. *Please, please, please. . .* I silently implored, but nothing triggered the wall.

I began to blabber: "OK, he's changed the lock, but. . ." I pulled the printed presentation from my back pocket and waved it at her. "I found this in there last time! Look! It's an evil plan by Pheel!"

I looked at the indecipherable sheet and felt the hope drain from me. I didn't need to look at Mum to sense her anger. I let my chin fall to my chest.

"Billy Benbow! Stop this!" she snapped. She so rarely raised her voice, I knew that she was super cross. "I know you don't like Phil, OK! I'm not blind. But all these silly accusations are just childish fantasy. He's not trying to replace your dad! He's just trying to be your friend. And you need to show him the same courtesy. Because he's not going anywhere."

And with that, she spun on her heels and stepped into the elevator.

"Come back upstairs when you're ready to be a grown-up," she said, and the doors slid shut. I stood there, stewing in my own frustration and anger: anger at Pheel for changing the locks; anger at myself for not guessing that he'd change the locks; but most of all, anger at the idea that I might be stuck, for ever, with a supervillain for a stepdad.

CHAPTER 11
"P" is for Pizza

It was Saturday night – pizza night – and it was just Pheel and me in the house. Mum had headed out about three minutes ago and Viv couldn't get here soon enough. I desperately wanted to avoid that "chat". The idea of a heart-to-heart with Pheel made me feel sick. The doorbell rang and I was up like a shot.

"Thank *farts* you're here," I said, yanking it open.

"Thank who I'm 'ere?" came the gruff response.

I looked up to see a red nose and round face staring back at me. It took me a second to recognize him in person. It was the mayor. He was dressed in his purple robes, medallion and a pointed mayor's hat. "You're not Viv..." I mumbled.

"Now then, young man," he said, peering over my shoulder. "Is your dad in?"

"Stepdad," I bit back instinctively.

"That's right," he mumbled, as if he either hadn't heard or didn't care. "I'm after Little Philly Pern." Then he took off his hat and stepped past me without asking.

I shut the door and followed him as he crept further into the hall, craning his neck up at the staircase and peering through doorways.

"I think Pheel's by the TV..." I began to say as he appeared from our cinema room holding a bottle of beer. The moment he saw the mayor, the mirth drained from his eyes.

He downed his beer in one and said: "Hello, Ron."

The mayor spread his podgy arms out wide. "If it isn't my old friend Phil Pern." He stepped forward so he was right in Pheel's personal space. "Phil Pern never learns, you know!" he exclaimed, giving me a conspiratorial wink.

I frowned. "Learns what?"

"Not to approach me face on, that's what!" he guffawed, before reaching up and twisting Pheel's nipple through his shirt. He exploded in laughter and I stifled a smile as Pheel stepped back, angrily swatting his hand away.

"Still doing that, are we?" scowled Pheel, rubbing his nipple.

"The oldies are the besties," replied the mayor, winking at me again. "Did you know, when we were nine, we twisted his nipples so hard the nurse made him wear a bra full of ice?!" He exploded with laughter again. "Little Philly's Boobies, we called them!"

I looked from the mayor, who was wheezing with laughter, to Pheel, who looked as happy as a bull in a rainstorm. I guess there's one thing money can't buy you: a new past. I felt a flicker of sympathy for him as a young boy getting constantly nipple-crippled. But it was blown away when Pheel reminded me of the man he had become. He purposefully gestured at his marble-clad hallway and asked: "What brings you to my mansion tonight, Mayor?" He put extra emphasis on the word "mansion", and gave a smug smile, like owning gazillions of pounds now meant he was a better, cooler person.

"Nice, nice! Look at you, Mr Big Shot Drinks Billionaire!" he said, ogling the shiny marble staircase. Then he looked down at Pheel and wagged a finger at him. "I've come 'ere to find out when *you* –" he poked him accusingly in the chest "– my old friend Philly Pern, are going to donate to my '*What are you doing*' campaign? Keep police numbers low, empower the average citizen. . . What's it gonna be? 50K? 100K? Whatever you can spare."

A brief, tense silence fell over the three of us. Pheel

took a deep breath, held it, and looked as if he was counting under his breath. Then his fists unclenched, his body relaxed and his fake smile sprang back on to his face. "Sure, Ron. I'll get my people to talk to your people."

The mayor did a little hop and clapped his hands. "You're a good man, Little Philly," he said, thumping him on the back. "A good man indeed. I'll see myself out." He popped his mayor's hat on, did a little bow and with that he was gone, leaving me standing in the hallway wondering what on earth had just happened. Why would he give so much money to someone he clearly seemed to hate? Probably just to show off. . .

Beside me, Pheel's demeanour had completely changed. His fake smile and try-hard eyes had been replaced by a quiet, controlled rage. I'd never seen him like this. After a moment staring at the closed front door, he turned his eyes on me. "Billy. Shall we have that little talk?" he said. It wasn't a question.

"Uh-huh." I gulped. "If you really want?" It felt like the room had suddenly got about ten degrees colder.

"I do. Let's go outside."

He put a firm hand on my back and guided me through the hall towards the Obserphatory courtyard. My legs felt weak. He'd never scared me like this before. But now I knew he was a supervillain. . . Had he worked out that it was us who had broken into the bat cave? Was he going to take the rage built up from the mayor's visit out on me and . . . I don't know . . . feed me to his crocodiles? I felt an urge to run but my legs wouldn't let me.

We crossed the courtyard and came to a halt by some marble balustrades. Pheel gripped them tightly and stared down on the neat grids of Blemish, all bathed in a hazy dusk. The smell of warm tarmac wafted up on the evening breeze.

"You must realize what this is about," he said, his cold glare still fixed on the town. "You must know by now."

I made a garbled, panicked noise that was not a yes or a no. My palms were soaking; my throat had closed up.

"Perhaps it's not a surprise to you," he said. "But I expect it is."

"Sort of," I croaked.

"I thought as much," he said. "I'm not who I pretend I am. People I tell this to find it preposterous."

"I guess it is pretty preposterous," I squeaked.

A brief silence fell. This was it: he knew I knew. He knew I was on to him. And he was surely about to do something about it. Something terrible. . .

"The idea of it seems crazy – absurd, even. But I assure you it is true," he continued. I squeezed my eyes shut, terrified at what was to happen next. I could hear him let go of the balustrade and turn to me, before saying: "*I* was bullied at school! *Me!* Phil Pern!" He guffawed as if what he had just said was more ridiculous than if he'd revealed that he'd been born an elephant.

What the. . .? My eyes shot open. Pheel was staring down at me, soaking in (and completely misinterpreting) the shock in my face.

He continued: "When I saw you the other day at school, with a banana skin on your shoulder and looking sheepish, I recognized it immediately. I felt for you."

Relief exploded through my veins. I suddenly wanted to laugh with joy! He hadn't busted me! He wasn't trying to scare me or feed me to the crocodiles.

It was far more awkward . . . he was trying to have a dad chat.

"I can see you're shocked," he continued. "Someone as c-c-c-c . . ." He wanted to say "cool". ". . . calm as me was *bullied*. But it can happen to anyone."

I wasn't shocked at all – not at the fact that he was bullied, at least. I'd just seen him with the mayor. Plus I already knew he was a grade-A jerk. But who cared? He wasn't going to feed me to his crocodiles! "Sure," I lied. "That *is* shocking."

He pursed his lips and took a deep breath of air, before gripping the balustrade again and turning his gaze on the town. His eyes frosted over and the menacing edge returned to his voice. "But what they don't tell you at school is that when you grow up, you can crush your enemies like flies." He raised an open hand and squeezed it into a fist.

He looked down at me, his eyes burning once more with that silent rage. My sense of relief began to curdle with unease.

"Walk with me," he said.

Something about his demeanour was making me

deeply uncomfortable again. We headed down the winding stone stairs and into the zoo. Below us, the killer crocs splashed and writhed in anticipation. A henchman stepped from the shadows and handed Pheel a bucket of meat that smelt sweet and sickly like it had gone off.

"When I was at school, I remembered every nickname, every snigger, every insult," he said, lifting an abnormally large chunk of pink meat from the bucket and hurling it through the night air. "And I used it to become the man I am today."

Platinum teeth thrashed and snatched at the meat as it hit the water. Pheel reached down to lift another chunk. I could smell it before he'd even raised it. But when he brought it into the light, my stomach did a backflip. Not because of what it smelt like, but because of what it *looked* like. It had a tuft of hair on it. But not any hair – what looked like HUMAN hair! I looked down at the bucket and saw a stray tooth, an eyeball. I suddenly felt weak and wanted to be sick.

Pheel threw the meat into the pen and turned to face me again.

"This world isn't perfect," he said, his face bristling

with dark purpose. "Not by a long shot. But believe me when I say I can change it. Believe me when I say you'll never have to worry about those bullies and their taunts. I'll make sure you and your mum are the most important people in the world, I promise."

I stood, frozen, staring into his eyes, as cold and deadly as two silver bullets. The fake smile was gone. The pretend cool was gone. I was staring into the man behind all of that – into the eyes of Mr Pernicious. And he was terrifying.

"Uh-huh. Sure," I croaked, nodding frantically.

Then he tossed the last hunk of meat into the pen and checked his watch. "Viv will probably be here by now, no?" he said, his fake smile springing back on to his face. "Let's go and put on a movie!"

"OK," I whimpered, and set off in a frightened daze back towards the Obserphatory, praying harder than ever that we could just find *something* that would show the world the real Phil Pern, before he fed anyone else to the crocodiles.

Viv was standing gormlessly in the front hall. Mr

Pernicious had disappeared and Pheel's try-hard act was back at 110 per cent. "Vivvy! Grab a bowl of popcorn!" He scooped a bowl from a side table and handed it over.

Even without knowing what I'd just seen, Viv still had a new-found wariness of Pheel. He cautiously took the popcorn, moving like he was trying not to startle a lion, and sat down at the opposite end of our huge sofa. I perched next to him, still feeling jittery from the croc pen.

"PholaCola, Viv-ster?"

He nodded and Pheel clapped his hands. A henchman stepped forward, cracked a can open and handed it to Viv. He gulped it down greedily, as if it would wash away all our problems.

"This is great!" said Pheel, slumping down on the sofa and stretching, his purple suit riding even further up his arms. It was like our chat had taken a weight from his shoulders. The doorbell rang and he jumped up. "That'll be the pizzas!"

Within seconds, a henchman had appeared with a tower of steaming pizza boxes. The waft of melted cheese filled the room.

"Mmmm mmmmm mmmm," said Pheel, smacking

his lips and reading the boxes. "Pizza House – this is your favourite, right?"

I nodded.

"It'll be good to try it out," he continued. "I'm supposed to be having dinner with a few friends in the Blemish one next week." He opened the lid on the first box. "Pineapple and ham! Hawaiian!"

He slung it next to him on the sofa.

"What's this one gonna be. . ." he said, levering open box number two. "Spinach and egg. That's a. . ."

". . .Fiorentina," replied Viv, his face turning a ghostly white.

"You're right. So this one must be. . ." Pheel prised open the last box. "Salami and chilli! Mamma mia! It's a. . ." The word hit me like a sucker punch. ". . .Vesuvius!"

Wide-eyed realization broke free of my brain and coursed around my body. Slowly and woodenly, I turned to Viv. He stared back, biting his lips, desperately trying not to blurt anything out.

"Shall we, erm, go and

get some, erm, sauces?" I asked Pheel, my face as tense as peanut brittle.

Before he could answer, I was off – moving at speed to the kitchen, pursued by Viv, urging every fibre of my body to try to look casual.

"Quick, in here," I hissed, pulling him into the walk-in larder.

I closed the door and the words flew out of our mouths like escaping steam: "THEY'RE TYPES OF PIZZA!" we whisper-shouted in unison.

"Pheel's presentation: it wasn't listing locations, it was a pizza order! Hawaii, Fiorentina, Vesuvius," I said breathlessly, hitting my palm against my head.

Viv was hopping excitedly. "And PH must stand for. . ."

I hadn't even got that far. ". . .Pizza House," I said, practically speechless. "Pheel said he's going there next week. That must be The Meeting! This is it! This is our chance to bust him!"

We both fell into a stunned silence as the reality of the situation dawned on us. We were going to have to infiltrate a secret meeting of supervillains in a pizza restaurant and gather enough evidence to bust Pheel. Spying on one supervillain had been hard enough. Now we had to spy on a whole bunch of them.

CHAPTER 12

"P" is for Plan

Viv was sitting in front of his bedroom computer. One hand gripped what looked like a laser pen; the other dragged the mouse furiously back and forth across its pad. He had something top secret to show me – or so he'd said.

"What's going on?" I asked, trying to peer around him at the screen.

He moved his body left and right to obscure my view. "You'll see. Just give me a moment."

I turned away and gazed out the window, my mind wandering back to last night and the mayor's surprise visit. Something about it still bugged me. "It was so weird," I said, still gazing out the window. "The mayor was soooooo rude to Pheel last night. And Pheel clearly hates him. And then at the end, he just agreed to give him loads of money. Why would he do that?"

Viv momentarily stopped swearing at his computer. "It's been bugging me too," he said. "It could be that he was just showing off." He tapped his finger on his chin. "Or. . . Remember what Mr Meringue said that supervillains did? Maybe he's handing out money to get the mayor's support and mask his more *devious* operations. Maybe he wants something from the mayor."

That must *be it*, I thought. But what?

Viv turned back to his computer, clicked the mouse some more, then let out a little yelp of delight.

"Right, it's working!" A 3D model of a building sprang up on the screen. "This took me *hours* to build." He clicked his laser pen and pointed it at the screen. "It is an exact replica of the Blemish Pizza House."

Wow. He'd really gone to town on his prep work.

He moved his laser marker to a large room at the back of the virtual building. "And this is the private dining room, where the meeting is taking place."

I couldn't help but be impressed. This was Viv in his element. Organizing. Plotting. Planning.

"And *this*," he said, moving his laser pen slightly, "is the balcony above the private dining room's all-you-can-eat salad buffet. This is where you are going to hide and spy on the meeting."

I focused and nodded. Inside me, trepidation mixed with an almost illicit excitement. He clicked a button on his laser marker and a photo sprang up on-screen. It was of the balcony – a slightly dilapidated wooden structure home to two white statues that looked down on the dining room.

"Mars and Venus," he said, then picked up his can of PholaCola and had a long slurp.

I squinted. "They don't look much like planets to me."

He rolled his eyes. "They're Roman gods, you dummy! The god of war, and the god of love. Good and evil." He bounced his eyes as if he was sharing a joke with Mr Meringue. I forced a smile and peered in closer. The god of Mars Bars was wearing what looked like an upside-down plant pot on his head, while Venus's breasts were almost spilling out. They were an odd pair (the gods, not the breasts).

Viv lifted a folded white cotton sheet from his desk and placed it on my lap. "What's this?" I asked. I stood up and the sheet unfurled, revealing a home-made white tunic, just like Mars Bar was wearing.

"Your costume!" he said. "You are going to disguise yourself as the Mars statue!" Then he pulled out a Dictaphone. "And with this taped to your chest, you can record the whole meeting!"

"Wait, wait, wait! Just how do you intend for *me* to look like a *statue*?"

He lifted a tub of white face paint. "For your hands," he said.

I raised a sceptical eyebrow. "And for my head?"

He grinned. Then he bent down behind the bed and lifted something, hiding it behind his back.

"I've washed the inside and stretched it a bit. . ." he began to say, then moved his hands in front to reveal the white bin that Brayden Balls had got stuck on my head. In the middle of it, he had cut two eyeholes.

"Ta da!" he said, placing it over my head. I peered

out through the holes and turned to look at myself in the mirror. I had to admit, it had a pretty uncanny resemblance to Mars Bar's helmet.

Viv beamed. "You're not Bin Boy Benbow. You're Mars, the God of War!" He gave me a double thumbs up.

"You know what?" I said, my distorted voice echoing around the inside of the bin. "It's not a bad plan."

Viv scoffed confidently. "Not a bad plan? It's fail proof!"

Suddenly, Viv's computer screen began to flicker and flash. He looked at it with a mixture of alarm and distrust. "What's it doing?" he asked.

I had no idea.

The screen began to dissolve and an image appeared. It looked like it was the video feed of a cellar. And not just any cellar. . .

We watched as the back of a brown boiler suit walked away from the screen and the rear of a tinfoil hat hove into view. Connie turned, sat down on her chair, picked up a magazine and began reading casually.

"What the. . .?" muttered Viv. "How's she. . .?"

Connie looked up at the screen and feigned surprise, as if she'd bumped into us in the post office queue, not hacked Viv's computer with a video stream. "Oh, hi, guys, I didn't see you there," she said, putting down her magazine.

I suddenly realized the bin helmet was still on my head. I frantically whipped it off and rolled it under Viv's bed, unsure if she'd registered it or not.

Viv, on the other hand, was more worried about the invasion of his privacy. "You can't just hack into my computer like this!"

She could. And she had. And I wasn't sure what he could do about it.

"You haven't called!" she said, giving us that maniacal grin and waving a hand telephone symbol around her ear. "I was just wondering if you still had my number." I did. But before I could reply, it flashed up our screen in big neon-yellow digits. "Just in case!" she said. Boy, you couldn't fault her perseverance.

"Sorry," I said, grasping for an excuse that I immediately regretted. "It's just, we've been really busy."

"Trying to bust your stepdad?" she asked, without a second's pause, then added: "Cos I'm still here to help, you know."

"No, just, erm, school stuff," said Viv, scrabbling for a close-window button that didn't seem to exist.

She peered in closer to the screen. "By the way, what was on your head just now? It looked real weird," she said, oblivious to the fact that she was wearing a tinfoil hat.

Farts, I thought. "Nothing, it was nothing," I blabbered.

Viv was furiously reaching for the power button now, and Connie sensed that.

"Don't be strangers!" she shouted. "Call me any time. Together we ca—"

The screen gave a click, hum and died.

Viv sat up and puffed out his cheeks. After a few seconds of silence, he said: "She didn't see the outfit properly, did she?" It like he was desperately trying to reassure himself.

I shook my head and did the same: "No. I'm certain she didn't."

CHAPTER 13

"P" is for Psychochemicals

I stood on the balcony, nervous breaths echoing inside my bin helmet. Viv and I had snuck into the private dining room about an hour ago, pretending we were two customers looking for the toilets. Then we'd stealthily removed the Mars statue from its plinth and laid it flat along the balcony. I'd slipped into my costume, then Viv had wished me luck and made his exit – leaving me up here, ready to spy on a council of supervillains that hadn't yet arrived.

I shuffled along the balcony to get a better view from its tiny window. They should arrive any minute. I looked at my white hands, and then the rest of my outfit. I was kitted out in a white long-sleeved T-shirt and leggings, with Viv's home-made tunic over the top. Beneath it all, he'd sellotaped the Dictaphone to my chest. All I had to do when the meeting started was press record and stay statue-still for about two hours. What could *possibly* go wrong?

The waiting was killing me. My palms were sweaty and I could feel my heartbeat going thud, thud, thud against the Dictaphone. I fidgeted nervously and the whole balcony creaked. I eyed it suspiciously. "Balcony" was a generous term for what was basically an old wooden platform reached by a rickety ladder. The room itself was a big old space that reached high into the rafters, like it was an old chapel or something. And this looked like it might have been where a choir sat. Now it was just full of boxes of old pizza menus and two dusty statues. Viv had been right, though – there was nowhere to hide up here. If I wanted to spy on the meeting, I'd have to be a statue.

An enormous ROARRRRRRR broke the silence and I glanced out of the window. A monster truck the size of a two-storey house pulled up outside the restaurant.

Its door swung open to reveal the robot I'd seen in the volcano. Lights flashed and beeped all over his chest, and wires snaked along his limbs. Now I could see him properly, Viv had been right all along: it wasn't a Halloween costume. It really WAS a robot.

It leapt to the floor with a loud crack of the pavement, as a shiny purple drag car pulled up alongside. I didn't have time to see who was in it, but I knew one thing – the supervillains were arriving. My tummy on a spin-wash, I climbed on to the plinth. Then, with a deep breath, I pressed the record button, fixed my limbs into Mars's pose and froze. It was going to be a long, long evening.

The private dining room door swung open and a spotty waiter led the robot and a spindly fur-clad lady into the room. Something about her fur scarf looked odd, but I couldn't put my finger on what.

"Hi. I'm Darren and I'll be your waiter for the night," said the boy in a nervous, squeaky voice. "What can I get you to drink?"

"OIL!" demanded the robot in a voice that sounded a bit like a Dalek.

Darren was sweating badly. "Erm. Olive oil? We have lots of olive oil?"

"ENGINE OIL!" barked the robot.

The fur-clad lady sidled up to Darren. "Sweeeeetie," she purred. "Keep what you see in this room secret and . . . it might be worth your while." She opened her black fur purse and £50 notes burst out. Darren stared into it, his eyes bulging.

"Yes, ma'am!" he said, standing up straight.

"Well done," she said with a wicked smile. "Now, tell me. Do you serve children's tears?"

Darren scratched his head.

"On ice?" she asked.

"Is it a brand of fruit juice?" Darren finally replied.

"Not to worry," she said, turning away from him with a face like she'd sucked a lemon. "Get me a Diet Orangina."

Darren shuffled off and the door swung open again. In shuffled the Professor and Lord Krung, who was perched atop a computer desk being pushed by another spotty waiter.

"Siiiick costumes, bruv!" said the waiter. "Is this, like, a work fancy dress party?"

"Put me over by the plug socket," said Lord Krung through his laptop. "I don't have much battery remaining."

"Metalania!" chimed the Professor, shaking the robot's giant pincher before turning to the lady. "And Madame Mink! How marvellous to see you. We are to have the most BIG news tonight."

"We are all *veeeeeery* excited to hear about the plans," she purred, stroking her scarf, which wriggled and squirmed. I could see what was bothering me about it now. It wasn't a scarf at all! It was dozens and dozens of black ferret-like creatures, all writhing and crawling around her neck. I gave a little shudder.

The door swung open again and in filed more supervillains – all of whom I recognized from the volcano. There was a giant powerlifting lady with a blonde perm; a plump dead-faced woman wearing a costume that looked like it was from *The Sound of Music*; a rake-thin man with diamond eyes and a pointed tongue. In total, there was a cast of about a dozen extraordinary individuals. And at the back, guiding them in, was Pheel! He was clad in his shiny purple supervillain costume, the silk eye mask wrapped around his eyes and his collared cape flowing behind him.

"Mr Pernicious!" said the Professor, sidling over to him. "What a wonderful venue! How very . . . normal!" He said it in a way that made Pheel sound really smart for booking their doomsday meeting in a pizza restaurant. "And is that an all-you-can-eat salad bar over there?" he asked, cocking a weedy eyebrow.

"Why, I believe it is, Professor!" he said, flashing his ice-white teeth and placing a friendly hand on the Professor's back.

"Do they have bacon bits?" asked the Professor, licking his chapped lips.

"If the Professor wants bacon bits, the Professor gets bacon bits!" replied Pheel emphatically. Alongside them, the other supervillains all set about exchanging secret handshakes and complimenting each other's costumes.

"Ladies and gentlemen!" cried Pheel, throwing his hands out in a welcoming gesture. "Please take your seats!"

The supervillains shuffled around the long oval table and took their seats. If it wasn't for the extraordinary costumes, they would have looked like any other big table of diners: some of them inspected the pizza menu, while others looked around for Darren so they could order drinks. Except for Metalania, that is, who began to eat his cutlery.

Pheel took the end place and remained standing. "Welcome, all . . . to the second meeting of the League of Villainry and Evil!"

The supervillains all drummed their fists by means of applause. Except for the powerlifter lady, who accidentally punched through the table.

"Allow me to introduce us all! Brenda the Immense!" he hollered. The room continued to drum as the powerlifter gave a nod of acknowledgement and sheepishly tried to piece her section of table together.

"Metalania!" The robot waved a pincer.

"The Professor!" He bowed his head in salute.

"Madame Mink!"

"Lord Krung!"

"Ophidius Fang!"

And so it went on. Until Pheel had come all the way around the table.

"And of course myself, Mr Pernicious! Thank you for welcoming me into your league!"

The drumming reached a climax as Pheel lifted his hands to the ceiling and then, like a conductor, dropped them to silence the room.

"First order of business! A new name!"

"Hear, hear!" said someone.

"It's been drawn to our attention that our current name, the League of Villainry, is not entirely ... inclusive."

Metalania coughed a Dalek-y cough and shuffled in his seat.

"And a new name has been proposed!" Pheel unfurled a piece of paper and read from it. "The League of Villainry, Evil and Robotics! Does anyone object?"

Lord Krung chimed up in his clunky electronic voice: "I think we should include a reference to the fact we are all equal. We are all in this together. Whether or not we have bodies. We all share the glory. We all share the risk."

Pheel stroked his chin for a second, then his face

lit up. "How about the League of Villainry, Evil and Robotics, *Syndicated*?"

The table broke out in a warm applause as I ran the acronym through my head and smiled: L.O.V.E.R.S. For a bunch of supervillains, they weren't super perceptive.

"All in favour, raise your hands," said Pheel. A sea of arms rose, including his own. "Eleven yeses. And the noes?" No one raised their arm. "Eleven yeses. One abstainer. . ."

Lord Krung piped up from the corner in his electronic voice: "I don't have an arm."

"I'm so sorry, Your Lordship!" said Pheel with an apologetic bow.

"But I vote yes," said Lord Krung.

"Motion carried unanimously!" declared Pheel, and everyone except for a sheepish Brenda the Immense drummed the table.

"Second order of business!" declared Pheel. "And this is the one we have all been waiting for! Drum roll, please!"

"Sure!" replied Lord Krung. Then he played an aggressive heavy-metal drum riff out of his tinny speakers. Everyone looked at him oddly. "Sorry! YouTube is playing up. Let me find another."

"It doesn't matter. Forget the drum roll!" said Pheel. "Second order of business is. . ." He left a pause like he was announcing the winner of a TV talent show. "Our plan for global revenge!" The table broke out in excited chatter. "If I can invite the Professor to take the floor."

"Ladies and gentlemen!" announced the Professor, bending in a crooked bow.

Metalania coughed again.

"Ladies, gentlemen and . . . cyborgs," he corrected himself, offering Metalania a conciliatory hand. "When we invited Mr Pernicious to join our little league, he approached me with the most deliciously evil plan. It was brilliant! Genius! I pledged immediately to do all I could help him. And to facilitate this, he made me director of his drinks company. This most delicious plan will be completed over two stages. And I am happy to say that stage one. . ."

The dining room door swung open and Darren staggered in with a tray of drinks. The room fell into an embarrassed silence.

"Diet Orangina?" asked Darren nervously. Madame Mink raised her hand and Darren handed her the drink.

"Oil, no ice?" Metalania raised his pincer.

"Twenty-six egg whites?" Brenda the Immense raised her hand.

"Beef soup with a straw?"

The room was so silent you could have heard a mouse fart. All the supervillains awkwardly pretended to read the menu or clean invisible stains off their costumes while Darren handed out the drinks.

Finally, when the tray was empty, he retreated out again.

The Professor coughed and picked up where he had left off. "I am happy to say that stage one is complete! We have incorporated secret addictive ingredients into PholaCola and it is now at maximum addiction! Children and adults all across the world are hooked on it!"

Everyone clapped. Pheel gave a bashful bow and stepped forward again. "We've put in some of the most addictive substances known to man. People don't just want to drink it – their bodies are *making them!*"

The room applauded as I desperately tried to contain my shock. That was why Viv was drinking twelve cans of PholaCola a day! I tried to stay still, but I could feel my heart pounding and the sweat trickling down my back. The Dictaphone felt heavier than if I had a cow strapped to my chest.

"And now, it is time to move on to stage two!" continued the Professor. "The addition of the psychochemicals!"

Brenda put her hand up. "What exactly are *psychochemicals*?"

"I'm glad you asked!" replied the Professor. "They are what you might also call mind-altering substances."

Now it was Madame Mink's turn to raise a hand: "And what will they *do* exactly."

Pheel stepped forward. "We'll get to that. First, let me ask you a question." He paused to survey the room, milking the anticipation. "What is the most potent weapon in the world?"

Metalania leapt to his feet, waving his arms in the air. "PINCERS!" he roared.

The rest of the room exchanged sideways glances.

"SORRY, I GOT EXCITED," he said, and sat down.

Pheel repeated himself, leaning forward with a conspiratorial whisper. "Think about it... The *most* potent weapon in the world?"

The room broke into muttered chatter.

"Is it nuclear bombs?" asked Brenda the Immense.

"Is it information?" asked another person.

"Is it mosquitoes? I think I read somewhere that it is mosquitoes," said someone else. It definitely wasn't that.

"No!" said Pheel, silencing the room with a swoosh of his hand. "I'll tell you what is the most potent weapon in the world. It's the very weapon that's been used against every one of us here: against you, Professor, when they mocked your fragile body! Against you, Brenda, when they poured scorn on you for not conforming to female stereotypes. And against you, Lord Krang, when they teased you for being too brainy." He winced and corrected himself. "I mean: for being too clever."

Everyone at the table had their eyes fixed on Pheel. He had them in a trance. "So, let me tell YOU what the most potent weapon in the world. More devastating than bombs! More devious than spies! The most potent weapon in the world is . . . LAUGHTER!" There were little gasps and mutters of agreement. Pheel was on a roll now. He barely paused to take a breath. "Don't be fooled – there is nothing light-hearted about laughter. It is a weapon – used to belittle, demean and humiliate. What is worse than being ignored, I ask you?" He looked around but didn't give anyone a chance to reply. "I'll tell you what – not being taken seriously! All through our lives, we have not been taken seriously. We've been laughed at, bullied, derided. We've had to fight for every success, fight in the face of laughter. When I said I wanted to start a global drinks company – they laughed at me! When Metalania wanted to become the world's most powerful cyborg, they laughed at him! When Lord Krang said he could live for ever as a brain in a jar – they laughed at him! Well now, the laughing stops!"

Everyone burst into spontaneous applause. Pheel hadn't yet unveiled his plan and already the room was whipped up to fever pitch.

"Professor – the serum, please!"

The Professor removed a tiny vial of black liquid from his jacket pocket and passed it to Pheel. "This," he exclaimed, holding it up to the light, "is our revenge!" He handed it to Brenda the Immense, who was seated nearest to him. "Please, please, pass it around. It's perfectly safe. The Professor, Lord Krung and I have been perfecting this serum for months now."

Brenda handed the vial to Madame Mink, who held it up to inspect. No light penetrated the jet-black liquid, which rolled and moved like oil inside its glass container.

"Yes, dahhhhling. But what does it do?" she purred.

As she spoke, a bead of condensation rolled down the vial and dripped from its bottom. With a silent splash, it landed on her writhing shawl. Almost immediately, a little black body separated from it, rolled out and landed lifeless on the floor. The room took a collective intake of breath as Madame Mink looked startled. She appeared to want to drop the vial, but knew better than to let it smash on the floor.

"Don't worry! Don't worry!" said Pheel, holding his palms up to calm the crowd. "The mind-changing effects of the serum are sadly too much for animals, it simply melts their brains. But on humans' bigger brains, it has a much more . . . *interesting* effect."

He walked around and collected the vase from Madame Mink. No one else appeared willing to touch it. "If drunk in sufficient quantities – no more than a tablespoon – this flavourless serum kills a part of the human brain." He smiled the most wicked of smiles. "And what does this part of the brain do? I hear you ask. I'll tell you. . ." He paused, surveyed the room, then exclaimed: "It processes human laughter and happiness!"

The room let out impressed gasps as I nearly fell off my plinth in shock. Pheel wanted to destroy laughter?? That was far worse – far more diabolical – than even I would have guessed!

"That's right – what better way to reap our revenge on a world that laughed at us . . . than by destroying the very thing they used against us! When we launch our new cherry flavour of PholaCola, every can will contain a tablespoon of untraceable serum! Before international governments know what has happened, laughter will have been wiped from the face of the earth! We are calling our plan. . ." He left a pause, then smiled like a bloodthirsty weasel. "THE APHOCALYPSE!"

There were more impressed gasps and another round of applause.

He winked and added: "Because you can't spell apocalypse without 'cola'." Then he flashed a smug grin.

Cue rapturous applause.

The Professor stepped in now. "After releasing the poisoned PholaCola Cherry at a most extravagant launch party, we will retreat to our mountain hideouts." His reedy voice was in a strained shout now. "Ready to emerge to rule a world that will be forced to take us seriously!"

The room broke into deafening applause. Madame Mink was on her feet. "It is genius!" she exclaimed.

Brenda the Immense followed. "BLESTYASHCHIY!" she cheered in Russian.

Then Metalania: "With me, fellow supervillains," he boomed. "MUWHAHAHAHAHAHA!"

No one joined in, but instead exchanged more sideways glances. Pheel placed a consoling hand on his shoulder and spoke gently in his ear. "Evil laughter's not really an appropriate response."

Metalania hung his metal head. "I have misread the room again."

Up on the balcony, my brain felt like it was going to explode. This was worse than I could have possibly imagined. Pheel wanted to destroy laughter and happiness??? I was sweating. I needed air. But I couldn't move a muscle without getting caught. The Dictaphone whirled reassuringly against my chest. I had all the evidence we needed! I could expose and put a stop to this heinous plan. All I had to do was get out of there without being noticed. . .

CHAPTER 14
Bacon Bits

Pheel stood up triumphantly. "Ladies, gentlemen and cyborgs. Let's eat!"

The room cheered as Darren burst in laden with trays of pizza, filling the room with the lip-smacking smell of baked bread and melted cheese.

"Vesuvius?" he shouted. Madame Mink raised her hand.

"Fiorentina?"

"Hawaiian?"

Phil, meanwhile, was ushering people towards the buffet. "Please, help yourself to the all-you-can-eat salad bar!" The supervillains began to manoeuvre over to my end of the room, a buzz of excitement rippling through them. I heard snippets of enthusiastic whispers: "Psychochemicals!" "Laughter erasing!" "Bacon bits!"

The salad bar was directly below me. Darren had taken to policing the queue. Brenda the Immense was up first and took two plates.

"Um, we have a one-plate policy at the salad bar," squeaked Darren, timidly.

"One plate?" she roared.

"Um-hm." He nodded, looking at his shoes.

"Well, how about this for one plate!" she bellowed, flinging one against the wall and gripping the other with both hands. "ARGGGHHHHHHHHH!" she screamed, straining every muscle as she slowly – and almost impossibly – stretched the porcelain fibres of the plate until it was about twice as long.

She held up the supersized plate in front of Darren and stared at him. "Huh?"

"I, erm, guess that's OK," he replied as she emptied a tub of potato salad on her stretched plate.

Next up was Metalania, who began to stack his plate with great pincer-fulls of cutlery.

"Excuse me, sir, but those are for, erm, eating with," said Darren.

Metalania fixed him in his blinking red eyes and shovelled about twenty forks into his mouth, sparks flying as he crunched down on them.

"MORE!" he cried.

Darren's head shrank into his neck. *Poor guy,* I thought. This was a tough crowd for a Tuesday night.

One by one, the supervillains lined up to tuck into the salad bar, passing directly underneath me as they spooned great piles of sweetcorn, pasta and bacon bits on to their plates. Each second felt like an hour. Nervous sweat was streaming down me. But so far, no one had noticed that Mars was actually a ten-year-old boy with a bin on his head. If I could just last another hour, I could get out of here with the Dictaphoned proof, and the the Aphocalypse would be rumbled before it had ever got close.

Finally, the Professor shuffled up to the salad bar.

"I hear you have bacon bits?" he said, his thin tongue licking his chapped lips.

"Yes, sir!" replied Darren, turning to the bar. Then

his face turned ashen. "Although . . . it looks like we've run out. Let me just . . . check with the kitchen."

Darren scampered off and the Professor impatiently tapped his foot while the rest of the group greedily troughed down all-you-can-eat salad and pizza.

After a brief pause, Darren's head reappeared. "I'm, erm, afraid the kitchen is out of bacon bits."

The room fell silent. The Professor was turning the same colour as the beetroot salad. "WHAT DO YOU MEAN THEY ARE OUT OF BACON BITS!?!" he yelled.

"They're just, erm, really popular. . ." offered Darren meekly.

"WELL, MAKE SOME MORE!" screamed the Professor.

"I'm not sure if they . . . can."

The room broke into pandemonium.

"DESTROY HIM!" yelled Metalania.

"Devour him, my pretties," snarled Madame Mink to her rodents.

"JUST COOK BACON AND BREAK IT INTO BITS!" yelled Brenda.

The Professor was furiously waving what looked like a sparking cattle prod and Pheel was begging for calm as Darren fled into the kitchen and – after a few minutes of Pheel reminding the room of their breathing exercises – reappeared with a steaming-hot tray of bacon, snipping each rasher by hand into tiny bits.

"Clever boy," said the Professor, coldly tucking his cattle prod back inside his jacket, and he began to sprinkle his bacon bits on his pasta salad.

Plumes of heavenly bacon aroma enveloped me, making my mouth water. But it wasn't just the buckets of water pouring out of my saliva glands that I needed to worry about. The hot tray of bacon directly below was raising my core temperate by about 20 degrees Celsius. Rivers of sweat now poured down inside my tunic, pooling by the sellotaped Dictaphone. I was beginning to worry that it would drip down on to someone when something even worse happened. I could feel the wet Sellotape beginning to give. It was peeling off me and sliding down my chest. And I was powerless to stop it.

No! No! No! I begged it to stay strong as it slipped,

slipped. . . Before I could do anything about it, the Dictaphone had slid down my belly, out of my tunic and was falling from the balcony. I watched it plummet to earth as if it was happening in slow motion. Down, down, down it fell. And then with a loud SCHLOP! it landed in the potato salad.

I squeezed my eyes shut in horror and waited for the pandemonium. But to my astonishment, the room just carried on as usual. Chatter. Laughter. The screech and clash that was Metalania eating his cutlery. They hadn't noticed! I'd got away with it. Relief overwhelmed me. I opened my eyes and peered out the bottom of my helmet. Relief turned to horror. The Dictaphone was poking out of the salad bar, still running. And there was nothing I could do about it. If I even moved a muscle, let alone tried to get it, I'd give the game away. All I could hope was that no one. . .

"MORE SALAD BAR!" bellowed Metalania, standing up and moving decisively, and rather clankily, for the salad bar. "DELICIOUS FORKS!" he barked, piling more cutlery on his plate. "MY COMPLIMENTS TO THE CHEF!"

151

Don't look at the potato salad! Don't look at the potato salad! I begged.

As he turned to leave, Darren sparked up: "Erm, excuse me, Mr. . ."

"METALANIA!"

"Mr Metalania . . . but why don't you try some of the *real* food," asked Darren.

I screwed my eyes shut again. I'd never met Darren. I'd only watched him graciously deal with a room full of hungry megalomaniacs. But at that exact moment, I hated him more than every single supervillain combined.

"HHHMMMMMMMMMM," said Metalania. "I'M NOT FAMILIAR WITH . . . FOOD."

"Try the potato salad!" said Darren. "It's got eggs in it!"

I mean, seriously? Was the guy trying to get me killed?

"I WILL TRY A LITTLE BIT," said Metalania, stretching out a pincer. "JUST TO SAY THAT I GAVE IT A GO, YOU KNOW WHAT I MEAN? I WILL TAKE JUST ONE. . ."

Metalania fell silent. My stomach did a backflip and I felt like I might be sick. I didn't need to look to know what had happened.

"WHAT IS THIS? HE IS RECORDING US!" bellowed Metalania, and in an instant, he had wrapped his pincers around Darren's neck and was lifting him from the floor.

The noise of chairs scraping and a chorus of alarmed shouts filled the room: "What is it?" "What's going on?"

"THERE'S A DICTAPHONE IN THE POTATO SALAD!" cried Metalania, his pincers tightening around Darren's neck.

"Spy!" "Kill him!" "Maybe let him get a final drinks order in!?" cried the room.

Darren's face was turning red as he struggled to breathe, his feet kicking wildly in mid-air.

Oh . . . farts, I thought. I'd really done it now.

I had two options: stay still and let Darren get his head ripped off by an evil robot, or move and get my head ripped off by an evil robot. And it wasn't Darren's fault that all this was happening . . . even if he *had* been over-pushy with the potato salad.

I had to do something. I squeezed my eyes shut, pushed the fear and worry far, far into the back of my brain and tried to control my breathing. I'd caused this. I needed to fix it. I opened my eyes, stepped off the plinth and shouted: "NO! IT WAS ME."

CHAPTER 15
Man (Boy) vs Machine

In unison, the room looked up at me.

"WHAT'S GOING ON?" cried Metalania, slackening his grip on Darren, who fell coughing to the floor.

"Who's up there?" demanded Pheel.

His reaction took me by surprise. How could he not recognize his own stepson? And then it occurred to me – the bin was distorting my voice. I was completely in disguise! I felt a tingle of exhilaration at the thought.

I didn't really have a plan at this point. I just wanted to a) stop Darren getting squeezed to death like a whoopee cushion and b) get out of there before I got squeezed to death like a whoopee cushion. They all looked at me, half with confusion, half with anticipation, like they were expecting me to say something.

"Erm. . . It was I who bugged your potato salad!" I cried, placing my hands on my hips and stalling for time.

The room broke into a furious clamour.

"The statue bugged the potato salad!" yelled Madame Mink.

"A fancy-dress ghost bugged the potato salad!" shouted Brenda the Immense.

"A dwarf with a bin on his head bugged the potato salad!" yelled Lord Krung.

And suddenly they were climbing over one another to get to the ladder and pull me to pieces.

Quick as a flash, I yanked it up on to the balcony, stranding them below. Or so I had hoped. . . A violent BUZZZZZZZ erupted and two telescopic pincers flew upwards, latching on to a roof beam. Then with a loud WHHHIIIIRRRRRR, they retracted, hoisting up Metalania so he could swing on to the balcony.

"NOBODY SPIES ON US L.O.V.E.R.S.!" he shrieked. It wasn't the time or the place, but I couldn't help but have a little smirk at their name.

He pointed his telescopic pincers at me and fired. I just managed to duck as they flew past my ear.

"GET HIM!" screamed the supervillains below.

I stumbled backwards, turned and bolted for the window, heaving it open and clambering out on to the roof. *Metalania will never fit through there,* I thought...

SMASH! He burst through the wall, leaving a robot-shaped hole in the brickwork.

Oh ... farts.

The roof space was tiny. Five steps in any direction and I would plummet from the roof on to the pavement. I felt the bravery of a few moments ago drain out of me. I didn't want to die.

Metalania strode towards me with robotic clunks. "WHO DO YOU WORK FOR?"

"No one!" I replied, stepping backwards.

Four paces and I'd be off the roof.

"THEN YOU WILL DIE!"

"Never!" I shouted back, not really believing it myself.

Three paces. Below me, a crowd had gathered on the pavement.

"I AM GOING TO ENJOY THIS MORE THAN A DELICIOUS BOWL FULL OF SPOONS," said Metalania, menacingly, and manoeuvred his pincers in front of him.

Two paces. I really, really didn't want to die. But I couldn't see a way out. What had I got myself into?

BAM!

He fired his pincers. They flew towards me and I instinctively leaned backwards to dodge them. I teetered on the roof edge as they snapped in front of me, missing my belly by millimetres. They snapped shut on my tunic and held there. I could feel myself leaning backwards, gravity wanting me to fall off the roof but Metalania's pincers stopping it from happening.

"LUCKY LUCKY," said Metalania, and tried to retract his pincers. But, for a split second, they didn't retract. They had got caught on one of Viv's tunic knots. What followed must have lasted less than a second, but it seemed to take a lifetime. Metalania's pincers strained, and then with an almighty *RIIIIPPPPPPPP* the tunic split in two. The pincers retracted at speed and we both toppled backwards. The world was suddenly

spinning and there was nothing below my feet. I groped for anything to hang on to, and just managed to snatch hold of the guttering with the very edge of my fingertips. Swinging like a pendulum off the edge of the roof, I looked down and felt sick to the pit of my stomach. I was dangling miles above the pavement, my body swaying back and forth and my legs frantically scrabbling for a ledge that didn't exist.

Metalania, however, hadn't been so lucky. With an ear-splitting CRASSSSSHHHH, he smashed into the pavement, buzzed, gurgled and then, with the sound of a dying computer, groaned and shut down.

The crowd was directly beneath me. "Let go!" "We'll catch you!" they cried.

My heart was in my throat. I could feel myself swaying with the wind, the remains of my tunic flapping behind me. No way did I want to let go! At best, I'd die. At worst I'd break my legs and Pheel would find out it was me who had bugged them – and then I'd REALLY die.

One by one, I could feel my fingers slipping from the guttering. First my thumb . . . then my little finger . . . then my middle and ring fingers . . . until I was suspended by just two index fingers. I begged myself: *Hold on! Hold on!* But I knew it was inevitable. I shut my eyes, drew a breath and. . .

The air rushed past me, my stomach flew upwards and I braced for the hard stone of the. . .

BOFF!

With a gentle crunch, I felt myself land on something soft. Soft and very, very smelly. . .

What the. . .?!

I opened my eyes. I was in the back of a dustbin truck! It must have been driving past just at the right second to catch me! I shook a bit of wet tissue paper off my fingers and felt like I could explode with joy! I hadn't died! I'd escaped!

I clambered up and stood aloft the pile of rubbish, my torn tunic billowing behind me, gazing back at the flabbergasted crowd and the sparking heap of junk that was now Metalania.

My whole body buzzed and tingled with elation as the dustbin truck drove obliviously on. I may have lost the evidence . . . but I was alive! In fact, I'd never felt more alive in my whole life!

CHAPTER 16

The Morning After the Fight Before

I awoke on Viv's bedroom floor. The morning sunlight streamed on to my face with a brightness that felt somehow new. Like I had just been born.

I stretched and felt each limb pop into life one by one. The plan had always been to stay over at Viv's that night. Which was lucky, because if I'd gone home reeking of dustbin, Pheel would have smelt a fish. Literally.

Viv rolled over and drew a long sniff over my sleeping bag. "You smell of fish. Literally."

I gave my arms a smell. "Yeah. It was that bin lorry.

I'll use your dad's back scourer." I guess crime fighting isn't all glamour.

Ten minutes and some sore skin later, we had our school uniform on and were headed to Viv's kitchen for breakfast.

"Morning, Mr and Mrs Burman," I said.

They were both transfixed by the telly and didn't answer.

"And to think: in our town?" muttered Mrs Burman, not looking up.

The TV boomed with the voice of a news reporter: "Wearing what appears to be a bin on his head, nobody is quite certain as to the identity of this masked vigilante!" *What the. . .?!* Viv and I exchanged a stunned look and huddled around the TV screen.

The reporter stood outside Pizza House, next to the dent in the pavement where Metalania had landed. She continued: "Eyewitnesses have described the moment the vigilante single-handedly fought and defeated what police are describing as a 'sophisticated robot'."

Suddenly, up on-screen, there was grainy mobile phone footage of ME fighting Metalania! The angle of the video was making it look as if I *threw* him off the roof.

"His adversary incapacitated, the vigilante made his escape aboard what many assume to be his getaway car – a dustbin truck!"

Wobbly footage flashed up of me standing astride the pile of rubbish, my hands on my hips and my ripped tunic flapping behind me like a cape. Viv's mum cooed in awe. "How mysterious!" she said.

Back in the studio, the anchor was holding his hand to his ear. "It looks like we are going live to an announcement from the mayor!"

The screen cut to a press conference. The mayor was standing, bleary-eyed, outside his front door, wearing a dressing gown and his gold mayoral medallion. Behind him stood Darren, looking slightly in awe.

The mayor cleared his throat as flash bulbs burst around him.

"This young man was witness to a most grievous incident last night." He gestured at Darren, then ushered him to step forward. "Tell 'em what you saw, lad, don't be shy."

Darren coughed and leaned into the microphone. "There was, um, a room full of strange people at Pizza House and I think they were plotting something against the town and one of them was an evil robot and he tried to kill me but someone with a bin on their head saved me."

The mayor pushed him aside and retook the mic. "Extraordinary events! This vigilante person with a bin on his head appre'ended the robot, as you might 'ave seen by now. The police took it into custody and partially downloaded its hard drive, the contents of which do prove this young man 'ere right. On the hard drive was none less than a poison plot! A poison plot against this town!"

There were gasps and another round of flashbulbs. A reporter shouted from the crowd: "Can you release more details about the plot? Should we be worried?"

The mayor shook his head. "No more news, I'm afraid," he said. "The hard drive was too badly damaged to retrieve any more detailed . . . erm . . . details."

Another reporter barked: "What do you have to say to people who might accuse you of cutting police numbers at a time when there is a poison plot against this town?"

He grunted and curled his nose in anger. "I'd say those people are idiots who should be doing more to look out for their fellow citizens, not blaming a mayor who's just trying to do his best."

There was another call from the crowd: "Do you have any leads on who this vigilante might be?"

The mayor rolled his shoulders and stood up straighter, his voice regaining its conviction: "I'll tell you who he is: someone doing their civic duty, that's who! Someone who wants to help out the police! Someone who has taken it on themselves to keep this town safe! I'll tell you who he is – he's an 'ero!"

A mischievous shout came from the crowd of reporters. "Would you call him a *super*hero?" There were sniggers from his colleagues.

The mayor thought for a second. Then he licked his lips, shrugged and said: "Why not? Print what you like."

Flashbulbs burst as he held his hands up: "No more questions for today!"

We all gazed dumbstruck at the screen. I could barely bring myself to say it, but . . . a *superhero*?!

The camera switched back to the anchors on the studio sofa, one of whom was scrolling through a tablet.

"Well, Sally, it looks like social media has *already* given this vigilante a name! Eyewitnesses heard a young male voice, and due to his unusual choice of headwear and getaway car, social media has crowned him . . . Bin Boy!"

"Bin Boy!" echoed an impressed Mr Burman.

"Well, you heard the mayor!" said one of the anchors, turning back from the live link with astonished laughter. "Looks like we have our own local *superhero*! Let's hope he keeps us safe from this plot. . ."

Viv's mum turned the sound down and blew out her cheeks. "What do you think of that, boys? Superheroes. . .? Poison plots? How extraordinary!"

I didn't know what to say. We both sat in stunned silence. It was all too much for me to take in.

"Come on, Viv. We need to go," I said, grabbing my school bag.

"You haven't had any breakfast, boys!" she called after us. But we were already out the door.

We hurried down the street, speechless.

Eventually, Viv said: "It's amazing! People think you're a . . . superhero!"

I tried to keep a lid on my exhilaration. "It doesn't change anything. Unless we can do something about the L.O.V.E.R.S., they are going to poison everybody and destroy laughter. We desperately need people to know that it's Pheel behind the plot."

"But the town loves him!" said Viv. "They're never going to suspect the man who makes PholaCola."

I ground to a halt and grabbed my best friend's arm. "On which note. Remember what we talked about last night? About PholaCola being mega-addictive?"

Viv nodded. "I promise, I've given it up. I'm clean. Not one sip today."

"Good," I said. "Because I'm going to need you at your sharpest in the coming weeks."

We turned into the playground and stopped in our tracks. Every single kid was gathered around a mobile phone.

I sidled up to Darius. "What's going on?"

He turned the screen so I could see. "More YouTube

videos of the Bin Boy!" he said, taking a long slurp of PholaCola.

"He's amazing!" cooed a girl in the year above.

"What a hero!" said another, giggling.

The sense of exhilaration curdled with an aching frustration. *It's ME!* I wanted to shout. *I'm Bin Boy! I'm important!* But revealing my identity would be the stupidest possible move right now. And anyway, who would ever believe me?

Other groups of kids were chattering about the plot. "My mum says they'll probably try and poison the water reservoir!" said one kid. "My dad says the same! So we're only allowed to drink PholaCola until the plot's solved!" chimed another.

Great. Just what we needed. Even more people drinking the addictive cola.

Brayden Balls lumbered into view with his cronies, pushing people aside so he could look at a phone screen. He soaked it in for a minute while everyone backed away from him, then said: "I can't believe I'm gonna have to defend this town against a PLOT!" His eyes grew bigger, like he was staring at an invisible stack of hamburgers. "You know what I'd do if I found those bad guys? HAAAA-YAAAA!" He did a mock judo chop on one of his cronies, but accidentally connected with his head, sending him staggering backwards into Viv. Brayden's eyes fell on the two of us.

"Look, here's the old bin boy!" he shouted, slobbering up to me. Then he grabbed my bicep and wrapped his thumb and forefinger around it mockingly. "No way this dweeb is gonna be any use defending this town!"

They all burst into laughter and Brayden pretended to punch me in the stomach. He didn't connect but I flinched anyway.

"*Definitely* not a superhero," he chortled, and moved on, slurping away at a can of PholaCola. I tried to pretend that I didn't care as everyone pointed and laughed. *If only they knew...* Rage burned inside of me, urging me to turn around and shout: "I AM BIN BOY!" But just as it was about to take control, someone shouted: "EVERYONE LOOK AT THIS!!!"

Suddenly, everyone had lost interest in me and were crowding around a single mobile phone screen, spilling their cans of PholaCola as they jostled for a view. Viv and I followed, burrowing our way through a sea of arms and legs to get a view of the screen. It looked like some kind of commercial, with loud music and loads of flashing graphics.

"It's just been released this minute!" said the person holding the phone.

The graphics came to a sudden stop and there was Pheel in his purple suit and sunglasses. The crowd screamed.

"Shhhhhh, everyone!" demanded someone. "He's going to announce something."

"Hey, PholaCola fans!" said Pheel, shooting them the double finger pistols from the phone screen. "I have some amazing news for you all. Right now, our cola is the safest thing to drink in Blemish! Which is why I'm extra, extra excited to announce that our new cherry flavour has been perfected and is ready for the public! I want you all to join me at its global launch party NEXT WEDNESDAY in this VERY TOWN! The mayor has let us host the BIGGEST PARTY OF ALL TIME in the town park! Free PholaCola Cherry for EVERY ATTENDEE!"

The screams reached fever pitch. Girls were hugging. Boys were hugging. People were crying. I swear, amidst all the chaos, someone was blasting an airhorn in celebration. Everyone was ecstatic – everyone except two people.

"The Aphocalypse. . ." I muttered, a chill working its way up my spine. "It's going to happen NEXT WEEK. We haven't got weeks to stop it – we've got ONE WEEK."

Viv looked like he might be sick. Either because he was worried about the impending Aphocalypse, or because he was going coming down hard from his PholaCola addiction. Probably both. "Oh no, oh no," he said, desperately surveying the sea of celebrating children. "What are we going to do?"

I thought hard. And I was about to admit that – at that exact moment – I had no idea what we were going to do next, when my phone buzzed.

"COME IMMEDIATELY. URGENT. NO HATS."

I held it up to Viv and he pulled a face. "It's Connie."

CHAPTER 17
We Could Be a Team...

Viv and I wound our way past the faded gnomes. Viv was muttering behind me: "She's not going to be any help. She's banananananananas." That's right. He put six *an*'s in bananas. He sounded like he was going banananananananas. I looked over my shoulder at him. He didn't look well. He'd gone grey and sweaty.

We were halfway down the path when Connie's front door opened a crack. Her dad's face appeared and scanned the sky nervously. Then he slipped out, closed the door and practically jumped on to the roof when he saw us.

"Oh, boys," he said, putting his hand on his heart.

"You scared me half to death. Have you heard about this plot? Against *this* town, of all places. Makes me scared to go get milk." He opened the door and ushered us in. "Try and get her out of her basement, eh?"

I wanted to ask if she was no longer grounded, but something about his manner told me it was a stupid question.

We made our way down the basement stairs. Connie was sitting in her chair, her eyes blazing with excitement. Behind her, YouTube footage of Bin Boy was playing, its reflection bouncing off her tinfoil hat. It wasn't the footage we'd seen at Viv's house . . . it was a remix. Someone had animated it with a comic-book style. **WHAM!** as Metalania's pincers grabbed hold of me, then a **POW!** and **KABOOM!** as he toppled off the roof and crashed into the pavement – all of it set to epic movie music. In the bottom corner of the screen, the page-views number was in the six figures and climbing. Bin Boy had gone viral!

"There are dozens like this and more being uploaded all the time, from every corner of the globe!" she said with a mischievous grin. "Any idea *at all* who's under the bin?" Then she wagged her eyebrows knowingly.

I folded my arms and maintained a poker face. "It could be anyone," I said.

She raised an eyebrow. "So you're telling me that I didn't see you wearing the very same bin on your head in Viv's bedroom?"

I held my poker face the best I could. "You must have been mistaken."

A green beam shot out from her desk and, before I could flinch, scanned me from head to toe.

"Hey!" I shouted.

"RUNNING DIAGNOSTIC PROFILING," said the

computer. "PROFILING SUCCESSFUL. FULL BODY MATCH."

I swore under my breath and gave one last meek roll of the dice. "Lots of kids my size. . ."

"AND FULL RETINA MATCH," concluded the computer.

I pulled a face. "All right, OK, it was me!"

She clapped in joy. "Ha! I knew it!"

My secret had lasted less than twenty-four hours. "How many people are you going to tell?" I asked. Beside me, Viv was suspiciously quiet. He'd sat down with his back against the wall and let out a sickly groan. I thought he'd at least be arguing with her by now.

"Don't worry. I'm not here to snitch on you," she said, pulling a liquorice stick from a paper bag and giving it a long slurp, so that black saliva pooled in the sides of her mouth as she spoke: "I told you – I want to help!"

I continued to eye her suspiciously. There was still something I didn't get. "Why are you so keen to help us?"

She flashed her mischievous grin. "I told you. I'm not allowed out. So how else am I gonna stop all those evil nutjobs out there doing stuff like reading our minds and worse?" She glanced up at her tinfoil hat, then back down at me. Holding my gaze for a second, she grinned, shrugged and added: "Plus, I like you. You need someone like me to stop you getting killed."

She offered me the liquorice. I took a stick and buried it in my pocket.

"Lots of people are worried about this plot, you know. You're the only one keeping them going into full-on panic." She offered a liquorice to Viv. He stared at it vacantly and shivered. "What's the deal with Sourface? He looks like he's about to chunder. Is he OK?"

I looked at Viv. He'd gone even paler. And I knew exactly why: he was coming down HARD from PholaCola. "He will be. But it'll take a few days," I said.

"Too bad," she said. "I mean, his personality isn't up to much, but I bet it's handy to have someone to help you." She gave an elaborate sigh and looked out the side of her eyes. "Suppose you've got no one now. No one to help you find a way to foil this plot. . . To hack top secret documents and find clues."

I looked her up and down as she sucked her

liquorice in her tinfoil hat. She knew something. The Aphocalypse was less than a week away. We had to stop Pheel and the L.O.V.E.R.S. any way possible. Connie *was* pretty nuts, but she was here, she was willing and she had obviously already done some vital digging. "OK. If I tell you everything – will you promise not to tell anyone?"

She grinned, then mimed zipping her lips shut. I took a breath and unloaded on her: how we'd worked out that the PH meeting was in Pizza House; how I'd infiltrated it dressed as a statue; how PholaCola was super addictive; and how they were planning the Aphocalypse for the drink launch next week. When I'd finished, a satisfied smile was wrapped around her liquorice stick.

"You don't look surprised by any of that?" I asked.

She swung around and grabbed a piece of paper, pushing it under my nose. It was a document with CLASSIFIED stamped across it in red. At the top, it had a logo that read: CAA.

"Civil Aviation Authority," she said. "I hacked their website this morning and found it."

I scanned the document, registering words like "CLEARANCE APPROVED", "NOXIOUS CHEMICALS" and then, with a jolt of surprise, the Obserphatory's full address.

"What is this?" I asked.

"It's aviation clearance for the delivery of a huge vat of noxious chemicals to your stepdad's house this Saturday," she replied. "It says that it is 'cleaning products', but my bet is that it is..."

"The Aphocalypse serum," I muttered. I stared at the document, then looked up at her eager face. "I need to get a sample of the serum."

She clapped her hands in glee. "Just what I was thinking! If you can get a sample, we can run a full diagnostics test on it!" she said. "We can break it down and trace its molecular profile and make an antidote!"

Behind us, Viv groaned and slumped down, his back against the wall. "Just one sip, please. Just one sip of PholaCola," he pleaded.

"No!" we retorted in unison.

Connie clapped her hands and the robot arm

appeared, holding a sample pot. "Here, take this," she said, then clapped again. The robot arm retracted under the desk and reappeared with a thick set of white rubber gloves. "And make sure you wear these. Just one drop of that serum on your skin could infect you."

I sat there clutching the pot and gloves, the crazy ambition of the plan slowly dawning on me. What had I let myself in for? I looked at Viv, who had his head in his hands and was groaning. I desperately needed him to get better so he could help me plot how to pull this off. Connie was a good hacker, but Viv was a mastermind when it came to this kind of planning.

Connie stood up purposefully. "There's one more thing! If you're going to take on twelve supervillains and their henchmen, you're going to need more than a thick pair of gloves."

She pulled out a tiny earpiece and handed it to me. "If you need my help." I stared at the little white bud. Did I want to place my life in the hands of someone as unpredictable as Connie? I'd much rather have methodical, logical Viv backing me up. I stuffed it in a pocket as she strode over to one of her metal cabinets, her brown jumpsuit merging with the dingy twilight and her tinfoil hat gently twinkling. "I've been working on a few things in my spare time," she said, fiddling with a combination padlock and grinning. "You know, I had to spend that ten thousand pounds I embezzled somehow..."

She pulled open the metal door and my eyes bulged in surprise. Inside – each one in their own specially lit display case – were a dozen or so DIY weapons.

She extended an invitational arm towards the cabinet. "Take your pick."

I stared in a sort of terrified awe. "How'd you learn to make all these?"

"You can find out anything on the internet," she said. "Let me talk you through them! This one fires out laser beams that can cut through steel ... or a henchman's head! This one lets off a blast so powerful it can vaporize a hippo..."

"Why would I want to vaporize a hippo?" I asked.

She shrugged. "Dunno. Maybe you don't like hippos. It can vaporize smaller things as well, though ... like henchmen ... or baby hippos..."

"I don't think I'm going to meet any hippos at all," I said.

"Okey doke," she replied, and pointed at something that looked like a portable smoothie maker. "This one's great. You're gonna love this one. It – get this – turns people inside out!"

"Ewwwww," I said.

"Take your pick," she said, pleased as punch.

"They all look terrifying," I muttered, and pointed at what looked like the least deadly item, a pair of white trainers. "I'll take those."

She picked them up excitedly. "Good choice. If you ever get in trouble, just tap the heels together." She threw them over to me. "Just make sure you're either outside or pointed at a window."

Then she pulled out a futuristic-looking gun. It had a round chamber at the end and a red tip to its muzzle. I looked at it and pulled a face. "Really? What is that? A flamethrower? A freeze gun?"

She frowned. "No. It's a water pistol."

"Oh."

"At least take it to wave around and look the business

if you have to," she said.

I tucked it into my belt. She grinned like a mad professor in the damp half-light. "We'll make a good team, you know – me, you and. . ." She gestured at Viv. "Sourface there."

I was about to agree. Maybe we would. But before I could speak, Viv looked up, fixing us both in his bloodshot eyes and letting out a groan that sounded like a dying dinosaur.

"URRHGHHHHHH NO! Here it comes!" he cried. "I'm going to be s—" But he didn't get a chance to finish the sentence before he emitted his own toxic serum from his mouth.

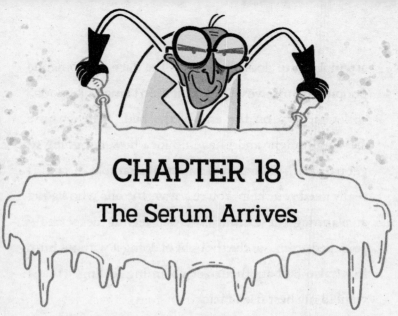

CHAPTER 18
The Serum Arrives

Viv didn't show up at school the next day. I badly needed his help planning how to snatch a sample of serum. I went around to his house after school but his mum said he was too ill for visitors. He didn't turn up the next day either. All the while, the serum's arrival got closer. And before I knew it, it was Saturday, the day it was due to be delivered. I went over to his house that morning and had to practically beg his mum to let me in. I found him lying in his bed shivering, his face the colour of old kebab meat.

"You don't look so well," I said.

He pulled a face that was either the face of someone

attempting to look brave, or the face of someone pooping themselves. Luckily, it didn't smell like poop.

I sat down on the end of the bed. "The serum's arriving tonight and I have no idea how I'm going to get past all the henchmen and steal a sample," I said. "I really need your help! You're always the one who's good at planning these things!" I was feeling desperate – panicked, even – at the thought of doing it without him. But I also had another overwhelming feeling – that I wanted my best friend back.

Viv began either nodding or shaking violently. He murmured something that sounded like: "Bin."

"What's that?" I replied.

"Bin," he said, louder.

"Of course!" I said, hitting my palm against my head. I *knew* he'd have a great idea, even if he did look like a zombie that's just run a marathon. I rummaged under his bed and pulled out the Bin Boy costume. Disguise was going to be everything! "Even when you're ill, you're still dead smart!" I said. Then I looked at his pale, sweaty cheeks and got a bit cheesy. "It's hard doing this without you, buddy. I need you."

He mouthed it again: "Bin."

"Don't worry, I've got it!" I replied, tapping the bin reassuringly.

"No – BIN!" he propped himself up and gestured wildly at the wastepaper basket. With wide-eyed horror, I realized what he meant. Before I could move, he'd grabbed my helmet and. . .

I sat on the sofa with Mum while, upstairs in my bedroom, my helmet sat in a bucket of disinfectant. However much I scrubbed, I still couldn't get the rank smell of Viv's sick out of it. It was Saturday evening and Mum was glued to *Antiques Roadshow*. The serum's arrival was imminent, and I was desperately trying to distract myself – even if that meant watching Mum's rubbish taste in telly. On-screen, a beige man was handing a pair of ancient knickers to an expert.

"These are my great-great-great-grandmother's knickers," said the man.

I pulled a face. If my plan failed, and this was to be my last few hours on Earth, I resented spending them in the company of three-hundred-year-old underwear.

My legs were fidgety. I couldn't sit still. I needed a pee for about the tenth time in an hour. I snuck off with Mum engrossed in the on-screen knickers, squeaking my way across the marble floor and into the loo. I lifted the seat and waited. Just as I was trying to squeeze a drop out, a voice drifted in through the window.

"I know, Professor... I know. It is a minor hitch. Nothing we need worry about."

It was Pheel. I flipped the lid down and clambered on to the toilet, pressing my ear against the cracked window.

"Calm down, Professor." I could hear a tinny voice yelling through Pheel's mobile phone. "I agree, it was unfortunate about Metalania, but his capture changes nothing. They have no idea about the Aphocalypse. In fact, it works in our favour. People are too scared to drink anything BUT PholaCola. With the serum arriving tonight, everything is still completely on track." He listened for a moment, the tinny voice now calmer, before taking a deep breath and replying: "I have no idea who he is, Professor. But I promise you, history will not repeat itself. If the Bin Boy ever dares to show his face again . . . I'll have his head on a platter."

Pheel hung up the phone and I leapt off the toilet seat and ran back to the TV room.

I plonked myself down on the telly as the gravity of the situation seeped in. The last time I'd dressed as Bin Boy, he was a complete unknown. Now he was the L.O.V.E.R.S.'s sworn enemy. And in a few hours' time, he was about to infiltrate Pheel's house and hopefully ruin all their plans. Talk about going into the lion's den . . . it was more like going into the lion's den dressed as a pork chop. What if I was caught? What if I was killed? The more I thought about it, the more fear and pressure began to overwhelm me. Was this me? Could I *really* pull this off?

Suddenly, a noise from above snapped me back to.

CHOOKA-CHOOKA-CHOOKA-CHOOKA

"What's that?" said Mum, looking up.

I knew exactly what it was. The serum was arriving.

CHOOKA-CHOOKA-CHOOKA-CHOOKA

"It's right above us!" shouted Mum.

I could hear a loud WHIIIIIRRRRRR through the noise of the helicopter propeller. It was the sound of the Obserphatory dome opening,

"SOUNDS LIKE PHIL'S DELIVERY HAS ARRIVED!" shouted Mum.

Out in the hallway, henchmen were rushing in and out of doors – a great river of black streaming to the Obserphatory dome. The noise reached a crescendo, shaking the walls as the helicopter lowered its delivery into the dome. There was a soft thud of the delivery hitting the Obserphatory floor and then the CHOOKA-CHOOKA of the helicopter rising back into the sky. My palms were clammy and my heart was gently pounding on the inside of my ribcage. It was here. It was real. There was no getting out if it.

When the noise of the chopper had finally disappeared, an eerie calm settled across the building. There were no henchmen in sight, no Pheel, no noise – just Mum, me and the knowledge that enough serum to erase the world's joy was sitting a few rooms away.

"Thank goodness that's done with," said Mum.

I croaked a vague reply.

On telly, the presenter announced: "I value these knickers at..." The knickers owner held his breath. "Fifty pence."

A deafening siren nearly split my eardrums. A red light flashed out in the sterile hallway. Mum and I clasped our hands over our ears as a calm automated female voice blared over the siren:

"SPILLAGE IN SECTOR SEVEN. SPILLAGE IN SECTOR SEVEN."

Suddenly, the river of henchmen had become a tsunami, sprinting through doors clad in full-body chemical suits. The noise and commotion lasted about a minute and then, like a passing rainstorm, the siren and voice abruptly stopped and the henchmen disappeared.

"Tch, tch, tch," said Mum, rolling her eyes, and settled back down in front of the telly, turning the volume up. I hovered uneasily next to her. Something wasn't right, I could feel it. On TV, some man was talking loudly about a vase. I didn't hear the footsteps enter the room. Mum did, though.

"I'm glad one of you are here," she said, without looking. "How do I get this programme to pause so I can go check on our dinner?" She was holding up the remote control and squinting at it.

I turned around to see a henchman. Except he didn't look like your run-of-the-mill henchman. He was even more expressionless than usual. His face was deathly blank and his eyes glassy.

Mum continued to inspect the remote. "Is it this button? Or is that for the DVD?"

The henchman moved steadily nearer. His presence made my skin crawl. He was looking at us but didn't seem to see us. The siren, the rushing henchmen; I instinctively knew exactly what had happened: he'd been infected by the serum.

"M-m-m-um!" I said.

"Yes, sweetie?" she said, engrossed in the remote like she was about to crack a fiendish sudoku.

The henchman staggered closer.

"S-s-stop!" I stammered at him.

"Not stop, just pause," she said, still talking about the remote. "Or is that the same thing? Oh, I don't know."

He was now just feet away from us. I couldn't pull my eyes from him. The serum's effects were worse than I could have possibly imagined. It wasn't just his happiness that was gone . . . but *all* his emotion. He was nothing; nil; void; a shell of a human; a ghost staring into an endless abyss.

I was frozen in terror. My throat was dry and the hairs on the back of my neck were standing up. I wanted to cry for help and then. . .

BAM! In a whirlwind of commotion, a half-dozen henchmen burst in and bolted across the room, throwing a bag over the henchman's head. Like a condemned man resigned to his fate, he didn't flinch as he was dragged out. In his place now stood a different henchman, one who clearly hadn't been infected.

"What was that racket?" said Mum, turning around with a confused frown.

"The pause button is this one," said the henchman, pointing at the remote, then putting his arms behind his back and standing up straight. "Will that be all, ma'am?"

Mum smiled. "Yes, thank you for being a darling," she said. As she turned back to pause the telly, she clocked my terror. "What's wrong, sweetie?"

My mouth opened and closed like a goldfish. "N-n-nothing," I said, and sank into the sofa. I could feel the fear coursing through my veins, but it was changing with every passing second, thickening into something else. It took me a moment to realize what it was. It was no longer fear. It was a new-found resolve. This had become SO much bigger than breaking up Mum and Pheel. This was about stopping a terrifying fate being inflicted on the world. Whatever doubts or fears I'd had a few minutes ago evaporated. I had to get that serum, by any means necessary. I had to become Bin Boy again.

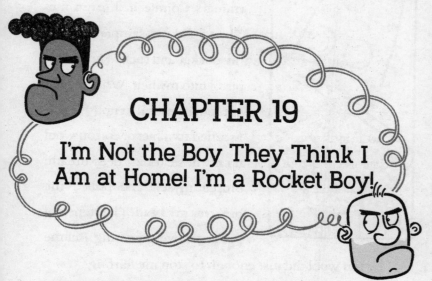

CHAPTER 19

I'm Not the Boy They Think I Am at Home! I'm a Rocket Boy!

On my bedside table, my clock read 23:59. So that I had an alibi, I told Mum that I was spending the night at Viv's – but instead snuck back into my bedroom and waited for midnight.

The clock ticked over. Quietly as a mouse, I slid from bed and pulled on my white trousers and white jumper. Next, I reached for my helmet. Even from an arm's length away, I could smell the stench of Viv's sick radiating from it. I lifted it closer to my nose, sniffed again and nearly wretched. I couldn't bear putting it on just yet, so instead slipped into the rubber gloves and

trainers Connie had given me. Then I slid her sample pot into my pocket and tucked her water pistol into my belt. Who knew if it might be useful or not? Finally, I stuffed two bits of cotton wool up my nose, took a deep breath, braced myself and pulled the bin over my head. The stench of puke was overpowering. But the cotton wool did just enough to stop me barfing.

I stood and looked myself up and down in the mirror. Dressed all in white, I looked ... actually pretty cool! I checked myself out for a second time. Something was missing... Something was different from the YouTube footage of me. It took me a moment to realize what it was. My cape! I ripped the sheet from my bed and tied it around my neck, then checked myself again in the mirror. A surge of exhilaration snaked up my spine and exploded into my brain. Trying to breathe only through my mouth, I said to the mirror: "Welcome back, Bin Boy!"

I turned and looked at the door. A wave of nerves

broke in my tummy. Could I do this? More importantly: Could I do this *and* get away with it; just walk out of my bedroom dressed as Pheel's sworn enemy Bin Boy and steal his serum? I could feel tendrils of doubt spread out through my brain, seizing control of my limbs. I looked down at my bedside table. There was one last bit of kit Connie had given me. The earpiece. I'd debated long and hard about this: How useful would it *really* be, having Connie in my ear? Could she even see what I was going to be doing? Would it be a help ... or the sort of massive distraction that got me caught? I glanced once more at the door, sucked in my breath and decided it was worth the gamble. I snatched it up, lifted my helmet and slipped it inside my ear.

"H-hello?" I said.

"YES!" A whoop of delight exploded in my ear. "Come in, Bin Boy! This is mission control!"

My footsteps echoed down the empty Obserphatory corridors as I ran from one corner to the next, sliding my back up against the wall as my heart pounded furiously in my ribcage.

"Connie. Corridor check," I whispered between breaths.

It turns out having Connie in my ear *was* incredibly useful. She had hacked into the Obserphatory's wall-to-wall CCTV and could warn me if there were any henchmen en route to the Dome. I'm not sure why I ever doubted her. . .

"So, when you speak over walkie-talkie like this, you always end by saying over. Over," she said.

Scrap that, I knew exactly why I doubted her – because she was still a massive gasbag, even in the middle of a mission.

"Over over?" I said.

"No, just over."

"Fine."

"No, roger," she replied.

"Roger who?"

"Roger's what you say when you have understood the other person. Over."

"OK. Fine."

"Roger. You say, roger. Over."

"OK, roger over. Now will you just check the

corridor, Connie!"

"No, just ro. . ."

"Connie, check the freaking corridor!" I hissed.

"Copy that, Bin Boy," she said, sensing the gravity in my voice. "Corridor 5E clear and. . ." She tapped a few keyboard buttons. ". . .tapes erased."

I slid around the corner, darted to the next one and waited for Connie to repeat her efforts, reassured by the knowledge that not only was she checking for henchmen, she was also wiping the CCTV tapes, so there would be no record of Bin Boy's infiltration of the Obserphatory. Like I say, why did I ever doubt her?

The last corridor clear, I darted to the side door of the Dome and cracked it open. The lights were dimmed. The huge space felt like a sleeping cathedral. And in the middle of it, a towering black vat – the serum. I could smell it clinging to the night air, a sharp, chemically odour like the inside of a science class.

"That's the mother lode," said Connie. "Let me do a quick recce of the Dome. . ." She tapped a few keyboard buttons. "Right, you've got bogies on the far side. Over."

I scanned the room and clocked two henchmen on the other side of the Dome. They stood with their arms folded, staring vacantly into the dome.

"There's no way I can get to the vat without them seeing me," I whispered.

"Copy that," said Connie. "Let me just. . ."

High up in the Dome, there was a loud bang and a shower of sparks as a CCTV camera exploded. The henchmen spun and looked up in surprise. "Go!" she hissed.

I dashed into the Dome, darting past a large control panel and hiding behind the vat. My heart was in my mouth, but I'd made it! I could hear them muttering about the CCTV camera. They hadn't noticed me! A steel ladder climbed upwards and hooked itself over the top of the vat. As softly as I could, I took hold of it and climbed, one rung at a time, until I'd reached the top.

"Come in, Bin Boy. What can you see? Over," said Connie.

"There's a small hatch into the vat," I replied. "I'm going to open it and get a sample. Try and keep the henchmen distracted. Over."

"Copy that!" replied Connie, as another camera exploded high up in the Dome to surprised shouts.

I gently slid the hatch open. Below me, the serum shimmered like dark evil. Its noxious chemical vapours made my eyes water and my nostrils sting. Gripping hold of the ladder with one hand, I removed the sample pot from my pocket and lowered it towards the serum, trying my best to keep my gloves out of the liquid. Slowly, slowly, I scooped a little up, pulled it out and then . . . my thumb slipped. Almost in slow motion, the pot squeezed from my grasp. My stomach churned as it landed, with a soft plop, into the serum and disappeared into the black.

I squeezed my eyes shut. *"Farts! Farts! Farts! Farts!"*

"What's happening?" asked Connie.

"I've dropped the pot!"

"Then find something else! I'll keep them distracted. Over." Another camera exploded, cascading sparks from the ceiling.

I desperately looked around the dome for an alternative – something sealable that I could store a deadly serum in. Another camera exploded. The henchmen were on their walkie-talkies: "Come in, control room, what's happening, please?"

"Hurry up!" hissed Connie. "There's only two more cameras left – and if I explode those, I lose visuals in there."

I scanned some more until my eyes settled on the water pistol tucked in my belt. *Bingo!*

I slipped it from my waistband and, wrapping an arm around the ladder for support, steadily unscrewed the water container from the gun. This time, I gripped hold of it with every ounce of concentration, dragging it along the calm black surface and scooping up the serum. Then I screwed it back into the gun, slipped it into my belt and clenched my fist in celebration.

"I've got it! Over."

Connie was shouting in my ear: "Right! Get out of there, now! I'll give you cover. Over." Another camera exploded.

I pulled the hatch shut, wrapped my feet around the outside of the ladder and slid down, landing with a soft thump. I felt like a racehorse that'd cleared the last jump. All I needed was to sprint for the exit.

"Connie, I just need one last diversion," I whispered.

"Copy that, Bin Boy. But you'd better make it. Once this camera explodes, I can't see what you're doing. You'll be on your own in there if you don't make it. Over."

I steadied myself, waited for the BANG and bolted for the door. By the time I was halfway across, the blood was pounding in my ears. Then I was just five steps away, then four, then three. My heart was about to explode from adrenaline and excitement. I was going to make it. . .

WHAM!

I felt the wind rush out of me. It was like I'd been hit by a car. Two powerful arms wrapped themselves around my torso, pinning my arms to my sides.

"Come in, Bin Boy!" said Connie. "What's going on!"

I couldn't even think to reply. My arms were pinned and the air was being squeezed from me.

A voice from behind my helmet boomed: "Well, if it isn't the Incredible Bin Boy. Just what do you think you're doing here?"

"Come in, Bin Boy! Did you get out? What's

happening?" shouted Connie.

I knew exactly what had happened: I'd been grabbed by one of the henchmen. He was gripping me tightly from behind, so that my feet dangled inches from the floor. I frantically wriggled and kicked as the other henchman stepped in front. "Helping yourself to a bit of serum, are you? Well, we'll see about that! Mr Pernicious is going to be veeeeeery pleased to meet *you*," he laughed. Then he clamped his hands around my helmet. "Let's find out who this so-called superhero really is!"

"No! No!" I cried, kicking and squirming even more desperately. If Pheel found out it was me, it would be the end of the world. Literally! I hissed into my earpiece: "Connie. I've been caught! Do something."

"What?" she said, her voice rising in panic. "Do what? I can't see what's going on."

The henchman slowly slid the bin off my head. This was it. It was all over. My life. Laughter. The world as we knew it. I squeezed my eyes shut and prayed, the noise of Connie's panicked shouts merging into white noise.

The helmet moved up an inch. Then another. It was

by my mouth. And then, suddenly, it stopped.

"EURGH! WHAT IS THAT SMELL?" retched the first henchman.

It took me a second to work out what was happening. In lifting it just a fraction, he must have dislodged a toxic cloud of Viv's puke odour.

"EURGH!" echoed Henchman #2. He gagged and grabbed hold of his nose. It was all the opportunity I needed. I broke free of his remaining grasp, spun around and grabbed my water pistol.

"Don't move!" I said, pointing it at them. "This is

loaded with serum! Don't make me have to squirt you!"

"Yes!" shouted Connie. "I don't know what's going on, but YES!"

Both henchmen snapped to and raised their hands. "Whoa, whoa. Calm down, son!" said Henchman #2, his eyes wide with concern. "Don't do anything silly!"

"Back up!" I barked, wheeling around them slowly. I edged towards the door. If I could just move a few more paces, I could slip through and be gone. I was so close!

"Don't shoot!" said Henchman #2. They were still backing away. But they were smirking. Then they shared a furtive sideways glance.

"What are you doing?" I cried, reaching for the door handle...

In a flash, Henchman #1 reached behind his back and pushed something. There was a series of loud clunks from the edge of the room.

"INTRUDER ALERT. DOORS LOCKED," said the female automated voice. "INTRUDER ALERT. DOORS LOCKED."

"Ha ha!" the henchman said, grinning.

I grabbed the handle and pulled, but the door didn't

budge. *FARTS!* I screamed to myself. "Come in, Connie! I need you to unlock the Dome doors! Over."

"OK, right," said Connie, without a great deal of conviction. "I just need to find the right system. Over."

"Like, now!"

"I'm trying, I'm trying," she said, to the sound of furious keyboard tapping.

I heard the crackle of Henchman #1's walkie-talkie: "Come in, Dome. Status report? Backup en route."

I didn't have time to wait for Connie to hack the systems. It was going to be up to me to get the doors open. "Step away from the control panel!" I shouted, waving my water pistol. They split apart and scrambled out of range, leaving me at the control panel, desperately trying to remember which button opened the doors. They'd pulled a lever . . . but which lever? I pulled one. A loud WHHIIIIRRRRR from above mingled with the sirens, and the dome began to open. Not that one! It was a red button. But there were about five of them. Eenie, meenie, miney, mo. . . I mashed my palm into one and the female voice and siren stopped. I felt my body sag in relief . . . until she piped up again:

"ACTIVATING VAT RELEASE!"

I looked with horror as a huge tap at the bottom of the vat twisted open automatically and serum began pouring out of it like a waterfall.

"WHAT ARE YOU DOING!" shrieked Henchman #2 in a voice of utter horror.

"OH . . . TRIPLE, QUADRUPLE, MEGA FARTS!" I cried, the blood draining from my face, just as. . .

OOMPH!

I was knocked to the ground, the water pistol spinning from my grasp.

Connie's voice was in my ear, shouting panicked questions, but they just mingled with the wordless screaming of my own brain.

Henchman #1 was pinning me to the floor as Henchman #2 frantically tried to stop the vat emptying.

"I can't turn it off! I can't turn it off!" he shouted.

A great river of the black liquid streamed across the floor, growing and spreading as it flowed towards a drain in the corner of the Dome.

I needed to get out of there. I had to get out of there. I wriggled and fought and tried to reach for the water pistol.

"Oh, no you don't!" spat Henchman #1, gripping me tighter.

The henchman's weight crushed down on my ribcage. I could hardly breathe. Across the floor, the river of serum was becoming a lake, and its edges were getting closer and closer to us. If the henchman kept me pinned to the floor where we were, we'd both be swallowed by it. I wriggled and wormed and groaned in panic, but he just pressed down on me harder.

"Turn it off!" he cried.

"I can't!" shouted Henchman #2.

The serum was just inches away now, its fumes almost suffocating. We had to move. I knew that; he knew that. He lifted part of his weight to try and move us both away from it. But in doing so, he relaxed his grip just enough for me to wriggle free a knee and. . .

BAM!

Now, I don't know if henchmen usually have kids, but it was pretty unlikely that this guy would ever be able to after where I hit him. Although, right now, that was the least of his problems. He rolled off me, clutching his groin and howling, allowing me to scramble free and grab my gun, just as the jet-black liquid oozed over him. His moans turned into blood-curdling screams.

I jumped to my feet and looked desperately for a way out. The deluge of serum had blocked my path to the exit. I was surrounded on all sides by black liquid, stuck on a little island with two henchmen, one of whom was now completely covered in serum.

"What have you done to him!" yelled Henchman #2, his face red with fury. I didn't even have time to raise my gun before he rugby tackled me, knocking me to the floor again. The impact reverberated through my body. In my ear, Connie was still shouting, but my brain didn't have the bandwidth to tune in.

"I'm going to kill you, Bin Boy!" he snarled, wrapping his arms around my legs so I couldn't get up. From outside, I could hear the backup henchmen pounding wildly on the dome's sliding doors, trying to get in. Connie's shouts were getting louder.

I desperately tried to crawl free, but he clung on tighter as the serum spread its dark edges towards us.

"Let go!" I screamed. "Or we'll both end up in the

serum." I tried to kick his shins but my trainers missed.

My trainers...

"...YOUR TRAINERS..." bellowed Connie. "USE YOUR TRAINERS!"

MY TRAINERS! CONNIE'S SPECIAL TRAINERS!

I had forgotten all about them.

"What do I do?" I yelled.

"TAP THEM TOGETHER!"

I wriggled and wormed and fought, trying to loosen the henchman's grip just enough for me to move my ankles together and...

TAP, TAP

At first, nothing happened. Then my feet began to wobble, then rock...

"What's going on?" cried the henchman.

"Are they working?" yelled Connie.

I had no idea. Would I know when they...

WOOOOOOOSH!

Suddenly, my trainers were spitting out sparks, then flames, then with another almighty **WOOOOOOOOSSSSSSH**, I had left my tummy behind and was flying horizontally across the floor, about a foot off the ground.

"WHAT THE. . .!!!!" cried the henchman, who still clamped hold of my legs.

"They're wooooooorking!" I yelled, my tummy trailing about twenty feet behind my legs, as I rocketed a few inches off the floor.

With an almighty crash, the backup broke through the front door, and suddenly I was speeding towards them like a bowling ball. They staggered backwards in shock before I instinctively lifted my neck as high as I could and began to arc higher and higher until I was shooting vertically upwards, towards the open dome.

"I'M FLYING!" I shouted.

"YES, BIN BOY! YOU'RE FLYING!" whooped Connie.

The army of henchmen streamed in below me. Some desperately tried to stop the last drops of serum gurgling down the drain. Others stared up and shook their fists.

"Ha ha!" I cried.

Henchman #2 was still hanging desperately from my legs. "Don't let me go, don't let me go!" he cried.

"Oh, I won't," I said. "I know exactly what I'm going

to do with you."

I rocketed higher into the night sky, until the Dome looked like nothing more than a cracked golf ball way down below. The chill night air whipped past my cheeks and the stars twinkled like camera flashes at the Olympics. It was AWESOME!

"WAAAAHHHHHHEEEEYYYYYYYYYY!" I cried as I flew to freedom, the only remaining drops of serum tightly locked inside the water pistol. "I'M BIN BOY!" The night sky took the words and whipped them away. Then I reached an arm out to steer and shouted into my earpiece: "Connie, direct me to the police station!"

CHAPTER 20

Victory Tastes Sweet

I woke up on Viv's floor, my head still spinning from the exhilaration of the night before. I pushed myself up and peered at Viv. He finally had a bit of colour back in his cheeks.

"I dreamt that I was sick in your bin helmet," he murmured, rubbing the sleep from his eyes. He was on the mend. Which was great news: I had him back to help stop the Aphocalypse.

"You've missed quite a lot," I said, and excitedly told him everything that had happened since he came off the PholaCola.

His blew out his cheeks. "Wow," he finally said. "You nearly died. Twice."

"Yeah, but I didn't," I replied, a little disappointed that he wasn't as pumped as me about it all. "Anyway, we've got the serum now. I don't have to put myself in any more danger." As I said the words, I felt a pang of regret. Last night, I'd felt invincible as Bin Boy. The idea of going back to being Billy Benbow made me feel a bit sick. It must be what Viv felt like coming off the PholaCola. But right now, I needed Viv to feel reassured.

He narrowed his eyes at me and I gave him my best "I'm not lying" face. He bought it like a discount bag of crisps. "Can we see if it's on the news again?" he asked.

I grinned. "Absolutely!"

I hid my helmet, earpiece and costume under his bed and we headed downstairs. Sure enough, Mr and Mrs Burman were glued to the TV. A reporter's voice boomed: "At first, eyewitnesses thought it was a simple shooting star. But a closer inspection quickly established that it was another sighting of the individual locals have come to known as Bin Boy. It seems he was being propelled through the night sky by what appears to be a pair of rocket shoes!" On the screen, someone had videoed me with a long-zoom lens. I was arcing across the sky with my hand held out in front of me like Superman, the henchman dangling off my legs.

"What happened to the henchman. . ." whispered Viv.

"You'll see. . ." I whispered back.

"We now go live to an announcement from the mayor."

Once again, it cut to Mayor Blarblorn on his steps; this time he wore his pyjamas with his mayoral robe as a makeshift dressing gown. "Late last night, our local superhero, Bin Boy, apprehended a criminal and transported him to the local police station. And I can reveal that police found a key card to the Obserphatory on his person!"

There was a collective gasp from the crowd of reporters. My heart rate quickened and I leaned forward in anticipation. Had they found out he was one of Pheel's henchmen? Could he have cracked and told the police all about the Aphocalypse? This could be the moment that it all came crashing down for Pheel.

"The suspect is refusing to talk, but I have here a statement from Phil Pern in regards to the matter." He unfurled a bit of paper and, as my breath caught in my throat, read it out slowly:

"I have never seen this man before in my life. I can only assume he was in the Obserphatory as part of a plot to sabotage the launch of PholaCola Cherry. We are investigating the incident further and wholeheartedly thank the police and Bin Boy for apprehending him before he could do any real damage."

I screwed my eyes shut in frustration. I tried to reassure myself that it didn't matter too much; we'd destroyed the vat of serum and bought ourselves some time. Time enough to analyse the serum and get Pheel arrested.

The mayor folded the piece of paper away and looked shocked and angry. "There you have it, folks. The plot was an attempt to sabotage the launch of PholaCola Cherry! What kind of dastardly villain would do such a thing? But, thanks to Bin Boy, that evil plot has been foiled!"

The crowd of reporters all cheered. Mrs Burman

clapped at the telly and Mr Burman punched the air and took a long, celebratory slurp of PholaCola. "Get in, Bin Boy!" he cried. "Imagine that – a plot against *Phil Pern*! What will some low lifes stoop to?"

I turned to Viv and whispered, "We need to get the serum to Connie ASAP. Keep it hidden under your bed, then bring it to hers at three p.m. Mum will expect me to go home and look concerned for Pheel."

He nodded. "Only if you promise me that once we've busted Phil, there's no more unnecessary danger, OK?" Then he looked at me all serious and sounded like he was about thirty years older than he was. "I don't want to have to bury you next to your dad. Neither will your mum."

I nodded and felt a little pang of sadness. That'd be the worst thing ever. I reminded myself why I listened to him: he was always so sensible. Then I slipped out the kitchen while Mr and Mrs Burman stared transfixed at the rolling coverage of Bin Boy and headed back to the Obserphatory.

I slinked through the front door. Sunlight streamed

through the windows, and the marble hallway glistened. Hiding in the shadows behind a column, Pheel was hissing into his mobile phone.

"All of it is gone! ... No, we don't have any backup! ... I don't know, we didn't think that this would happen! ... No, we can't make more quickly unless we have a sample to replicate...! I don't know – he wiped all the CCTV... I WANT SOMEONE TO FIND ME THAT BIN BOY!!"

He clocked me and hung up. I nodded a hello, concealed a little victory smirk and strutted through to the kitchen like a prize cockerel.

"Hi, Mum!" I said.

She was wiping the surfaces in the Obserphatory's shiny white kitchen. The whole atmosphere in the house was tense. "Hi, sweetie," she said. "You've slept in late."

In all the fuss, no one had noticed I was missing. I pulled a carton of orange juice from the fridge and unscrewed the top.

"There's been a bit of commotion in the night," she said, tidying things into a drawer anxiously. "Someone has sabotaged Phil's new PholaCola flavour." She stopped wiping the counters and looked at me with her concerned face. "Be careful at the moment, won't you? I can't imagine why anyone would target Pheel like this. Or why anyone would want to poison *our* town – all at a time when there are less police on the streets. It's dangerous out there – we need to look out for each other."

"Sure thing," I said. "I'll, erm, look out for any bad guys."

"Thanks," she said, then continued wiping. "And it looks like Pheel might have to delay the launch."

I clenched my fist and wanted to do a little dance in celebration. Instead, I pulled my best sad face. "Oh, what a shame," I said, hiding a smirk as I gulped orange juice straight from the bottle.

Pheel stomped into the kitchen in a fluster. "Have you seen my rocket car keys?" he snapped.

"Where did you leave them last?" asked Mum.

"Here, on this counter!" he huffed. "You must have tidied them away!"

Mum opened and closed a few drawers. "I don't

think I have."

Pheel was more tightly coiled than a Slinky. "Yes you have, you always do this!"

I'd never seen them fight before. Mum was on the defensive now. "Don't speak to me like that." she said, her voice calm but taut. "Don't you dare take this out on me."

He huffed and spun on his heels. "I just wish everyone would leave my stuff alone," he shout-muttered, and stormed out the kitchen, leaving Mum angrily scrubbing the kitchen counter.

I wasn't sure what to think about their argument. I really didn't like seeing Mum upset, but I HATED every moment that she spent thinking Pheel was a great guy.

After a long pause, I said, softly: "You know, Mum, you don't have to put up with that."

She didn't reply. She just kept scrubbing the counter.

CHAPTER 21
A Big Hitch

Viv and I stood in Connie's basement, watching more YouTube footage of Bin Boy. Amongst the new viral videos, there was even footage of kids re-enacting my adventures with bins on their heads – in Japan, Brazil, Australia. Bin Boy was an international sensation!

In our town, however, the mood was different. Connie flicked on to our local news channel, where a reporter stood outside a supermarket.

"News of a poison plot against none other than PholaCola magnate Phil Pern has sent this town into shock," he said into his microphone. "I'm here to see how ordinary townspeople are reacting to the news."

The supermarket doors swooshed open and a man lumbered through, pushing a trolley.

"Excuse me, sir," said the reporter. "But in light of last night's events, are you worried about drinking PholaCola?"

The man pushed his chin in and looked at the reporter as if he'd just been asked whether he lived on the moon. "Course not!" he barked. "I've gone in and bought four crates of the stuff in solidarity!" He popped a can, slurped it down and headed off into the car park.

The doors swooshed open again, and who should walk out but Brayden Balls, a can of PholaCola in his hairy knuckles. He didn't even wait for the reporter to ask a question before leaning into the mic.

"Bad luck, bad guys," he said, internalizing a burp, then sticking his tongue into his bottom lip. "Looks like your stupid plan failed. And if you wanna try again, you're gonna have to get through me first." He sniffed, walked away from the mic before remembering something and leaning back in: "And my cousin knows Bin Boy, so anyone wanting to get an autograph should come pay me."

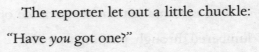

The reporter let out a little chuckle: "Have *you* got one?"

"Course!" he snorted. "I've got all the superheroes' autographs. Batman, Superman, the Hulk, Bin Boy. . ."

Connie stopped the footage, leaned back in her swivel chair, put her hands behind her head and gave me a long, pleased look.

The mixture of emotions swirling through me was more confusing than a fish-finger trifle. Half of it was frustration: the whole town was rallying around Pheel at a time when he was secretly trying to poison them. But the other half was pure exhilaration: I'd gone from being a nobody to being the most talked about person . . . in the world!

Finally, Connie said with a satisfied grin: "Next mission, we gotta think of a way of giving me visuals as well as audio."

"Next time?" I asked, with a flicker of excitement.

"Next time?" repeated Viv, with about as much excitement as a sleet storm.

She nodded. "Yeah! You know, whenever we team up again to make sure Bin Boy defeats those goons for good." She shrugged. "Or whatever other adventure we go on." She looked into the distance dreamily, like she was imagining some future escapade.

For a second, she sucked me along with her enthusiasm. I thought back to the exhilaration I'd felt when I defeated Metalania, and to the feeling of the wind whipping past my cheeks as I flew through the air last night. And I thought of everyone – even Brayden Balls – worshipping me. Viv gave a loud cough and the memories burst like a bubble on a lawn. I remembered what I promised him: no more unnecessary danger. This wasn't about me; this was about saving the world and getting rid of Pheel. That was all. I arranged my face so that it looked deadly serious.

"There's, er, not going to be a next time." The words pained me. But they were right.

Connie's face dropped. "What are you talking about? I thought ... you know ... we could..." Her disappointment was palpable. "We were great last night."

I looked at my shoes and forced the words out of my mouth. "We've got what we needed. We can analyse that serum, then we can give it to the police to bust Pheel."

She looked crestfallen. "Really? We were going to be a team ... us three. We were going to analyse it and make an antidote ... not just give it to the police. They're rubbish! They've had their numbers cut! There's barely enough of them to sing a duet any more, let alone analyse a deadly, traceless serum! You're a superhero now – you can't just quit!"

I pursed my lips, swallowed my ego and said nothing. Next to me, Viv looked puzzled. "I don't remember agreeing to be a team. When did we say we'd be a team?"

Connie's face frosted over and she folded her arms. "When you were being sick on my floor, Sourface, that's when!"

Viv drew a sharp intake of breath. Things were heating up. He finally snapped: "You mean, when you were hatching a plan that nearly got Billy killed? Pheel wants Bin Boy dead!"

"Me nearly get him killed? You're the one who had him get in a fight with an evil robot! He needed me to stop him getting killed last night!"

Viv wasn't backing down. "Yeah? Well, he needs me more: to stop him getting killed swanning about as Bin Boy in the future. Enough is enough. Billy's not a superhero. We're not a team. And there's no point going to all this trouble to stop him having to move to the Alps if he's going to end up dead!"

Connie scrunched her face up and looked away.

It broke my heart to say it, but... "Viv's right, you know. Bin Boy isn't a superhero. He's just me in a silly costume."

Connie was still looking the other way. "Yeah? Well, what do you think all superheroes are?"

The sentence hung in the air for a moment, until finally – softly – I tried to make her see sense: "It's too dangerous. Let's just analyse the sample and take it to the police."

"Be my guest!" She waved her hand dismissively at a nearby shelf. "All the equipment and software is over there. Take it away. Knock yourself out."

"Take it away? But I thought you were going to analyse it?" I asked.

She shrugged angrily. "Why should I? You heard old Sourface there: *'We're not a team.'*"

Viv began flapping angrily. "Please! Come on! Don't be so selfish! You can't let them destroy laughter!"

Connie exhaled through her nose, then looked around her basement. "Yeah? Well, can't say I'll miss it."

She spun around so her back was to us. I screwed my eyes shut in frustration. Great, just what we needed – Connie throwing her toys out of the pram at such a critical time. Whatever it was she wanted from us – some excitement, maybe? A life outside her basement? Some crime-fighting partners? – it wasn't our job to fulfil it. Right now, our job was to save laughter, not make her happy.

I eyeballed the equipment cagily. "Viv, reckon you can get it working?"

He took a deep breath and moved his mouth to one side in thought. "I mean, I can give it a try. . ."

"We'll have to do it at your house," I said. "If Pheel finds it in my bedroom it'll be game over."

Viv stayed silent while he wrestled with the dilemma. This was the kind of danger he liked to keep at arm's length. A very LONG arm's length. But maybe because he desperately wanted to bust Pheel, or maybe because his PholaCola comedown had left him too weak to argue, he grudgingly agreed: "OK, let's do it at mine."

"Thanks," I said, and we reluctantly loaded it into our arms and headed upstairs.

As my foot lifted on to the first step, Connie called after us. "You've missed a great opportunity! You're gonna always regret what Bin Boy could have been!"

I hunched my shoulders and climbed the rest of the stairs in silence.

CHAPTER 22

Oh, What a Beauti-Pheel Morning!

I got home to find Mum very subdued. Pheel didn't come home at all that evening. His rocket car was still gone when I went to bed. I slept with my fingers crossed that I'd never see him again. Hopefully, Viv would crack the serum tomorrow and the police would track him down and lock him up.

So when I woke up the next morning, the sunlight streaming through my curtains, and looked down from my fourth-floor window at the garage, my heart sank. His car was back.

I pulled on some clothes and headed downstairs. A

chirpy whistle echoed up the vast marble staircase. It sounded like a very out-of-tune version of "Oh, What a Beautiful Mornin'".

I shuffled into the kitchen cautiously.

"Hello, sunshine!" chimed Pheel. Then he poured himself a giant glass of orange juice and took a gulp. His crocodile smile curved like a new moon from behind the bottle top. I felt it in the pit of my tummy: something had changed.

I poured myself a bowl of cornflakes. "You're very happy," I said, narrowing my eyes.

"Too right!" he replied, patting me on the back.

I shovelled a crunchy spoonful of cornflakes into my mouth as he opened the fridge and dug around in it. "What's happened?"

He turned around and was holding a can of PholaCola Cherry. My eyes bulged. An enormous, self-satisfied grin spread across his face. "We've worked flat out and managed to produce a whole new batch of cherry flavour! THE LAUNCH IS BACK ON!!"

I sprayed cornflakes across the table. What? How?

But they'd lost all the serum! It would take weeks to replace – I'd heard him saying so on the phone!

He saw the cornflake explosion and thought I'd done it out of excitement. "Glad you're as pumped as me, buddy!" he said.

I grasped for anything. "B-b-but, what about the plot? It's too dangerous, surely? Someone is trying to poison the town!" I said the last words through gritted teeth.

Pheel gave a dismissive wave of his hand. "Don't worry about that! We're putting extra security around the perimeter. You're not gonna get poisoned, buddy!"

He ruffled my hair and put the PholaCola can in the fridge. Then, before I knew it, he was pulling up a chair next to me. He leaned in so he was right next to my face. I could smell his hot, sour breath as he began whispering, like he was sharing a dirty secret. "Say, buddy, what do you, erm, know about Viv's dad? About what he does for a living?"

Fresh chills worked their way up my spine. What was he getting at? "He's a policeman," I replied.

"That's what I thought. And has he, erm, ever

come round here to pick Viv up and . . . gone snooping around?"

A horrible feeling began to gnaw away at me; a feeling that I knew what this was about. "Snooping around?" I asked.

"Yeah, around the house . . . down in the wine cellar, maybe."

I was getting heart palpitations now. I scanned his face. The overacted merriment had gone. Mr Pernicious's steely grey eyes bored into me.

"No. Never," I replied.

Pheel straightened up. "OK, not to worry." And his jauntiness returned.

"W-w-why do you ask?"

Pheel rolled his shoulders like a boxer about to go into a fight. "It's just, I found something in the cellar. Somewhere . . . secret. And I traced it back to Viv's dad's computer."

The chill shot up my spine and exploded into my brain. Pheel had traced the police database list back to Viv's dad!

"But don't worry," continued Pheel, clicking his neck and turning to leave. "I've taken care of it."

Taken care of it? How had he taken care of it? Suddenly my brain was swamped with unthinkable thoughts. I pushed my cornflakes aside and jumped to my feet as Pheel strolled off into the corridor, his hands in his pockets, whistling badly. I had to find Viv! I had to check he was OK! If Pheel had even laid one finger on him, I'd ... I'd ... I didn't know what I'd do...

CHAPTER 23

Aphocalypse Soon

I stood in the playground, desperately praying that Viv would be the next person to breeze in. All of my texts to him had gone unanswered, and all of my calls had rung through. I stared at the gates more in hope than expectation.

Nearby, a bunch of kids talked excitedly about the launch. "I'm definitely going!" "My dad says it'll be the safest place in town!" "It's gonna make me SOOOOO HAPPY when I sip that cherry flavour."

The last few kids trickled in and the caretaker closed the gates. Viv hadn't turned up. The sickness deep in the pit of my tummy grew bigger. I just *knew* something had happened to him.

For the rest of the school day, every second felt like an hour. I sat and ate lunch alone, like I did every day when Viv was ill; my head swam with terrifying thoughts. I needed a friend more than ever. I pulled out my phone and scrolled down to Connie's number. My finger hovered over the compose-message button. Was she still angry with me? Would she reply? Would she even *care* that Viv had vanished? But then again, she was the only person who knew what was really going on – the only person who understood the stakes. I tapped in a message:

Need help – Viv's vanished

I could see she'd read it immediately. But no reply came.

I tried one more text: **Pleaaase! I don't know what to do. Everything's going wrong. I need your help**

Another pause. Then I could see she was typing.

What do you want me to do? she replied.

I could see she'd read it. For the rest of lunch, I checked my phone every twenty seconds. But no reply came.

When the bell eventually rang, I was out the front door in a flash, bowling past kids still talking about tomorrow's launch; running as fast as I could for Viv's house.

I swung around the corner on to his street, still uncertain if Connie would come or not. But halfway down, I could see her tinfoil hat twinkling in the afternoon sun. She approached, shoulders hunched around her ears.

"You came!" I said, catching my breath.

She forced a smile and didn't reply. She was pale, sweaty and anxiously surveying the street. Was she still angry with me? I looked her up and down one more time. No. Something was up, but it wasn't anger.

"Are you OK?"

She nodded, then said: "Let's get this over with. What do you want to do?"

I didn't have time to find out what was bugging her. "Let's check Viv's house," I said, marching ahead down the street.

She scurried after, staying close.

As his front door hove into view, my stomach sank into my socks. There was police tape around his smashed front door. I sprinted over, ducking under it and into his hallway. Connie hurried in my wake.

From the ransacked front hall, I could see Viv's mum sitting, sobbing at the kitchen table, talking to two policemen. Around her, the floor was littered with smashed plates and splintered chairs. I hid behind the door frame and listened in.

One of the policemen was small and bald and the other fat and hairy. They were listening to Mrs Burman through narrowed eyes.

"I thought they were just Jehovah's Witnesses or something," she said, dabbing her eyes with a tissue.

"Mmmm-hmmm," replied the bald policeman, coldly scribbling in his notebook. "And, erm, what did these 'Jehovah's Witnesses' look like?"

Mrs Burman sniffed and thought for a second. "One

was a huge blonde woman. She spoke with a Russian accent, I think. She was wearing what looked like a wrestling suit."

"Mmm-hmmm," replied the bald policeman, showing no emotion.

"And the other was thin as a biro. She had a fur shawl on that almost seemed to . . . I know it sounds crazy, but . . . it almost seemed to move!"

My breath caught in my throat. I'd recognize those descriptions anywhere.

"Madame Mink and Brenda the Immense!" I said, turning to Connie, who didn't seem to hear. In fact, she wasn't even concentrating on Mrs Burman. I didn't get what was up with her. Was it the kidnapping? The policemen? What was making her so nervous?

Mrs Burman sobbed into her tissue and the two policemen exchanged a quick, amused glance. "And when did these two *characters* break down your front door?" asked the fat policeman.

"When I wouldn't let them in!" she blubbed. "Then the big one grabbed Sanjay and the thin one strode upstairs. I heard a scream and before I knew it, she was marching out of the front door with Viv under her arm. She dragged him into a long purple car. The big one bundled Sanjay in and WOOSH! they were gone."

I squeezed my eyes shut in horror. My worst fears had come true. "It's the L.O.V.E.R.S. – they've kidnapped Viv."

Connie didn't reply. Then she whispered, partly to herself, partly to me: "I was wrong. I can't do this." She was backing away down the hall.

"Don't be scared of them," I whispered back, reaching out to grab her arm but finding her out of reach. What was up with her? She was normally so fearless. . .

"It's not them," she said, backing through the police tape and into the street. "It's . . ." She looked around at the house, the street, the sky. ". . . this." And then she turned and fled.

What?! I wanted to shout. *What's "this"?* But she was gone. For a split second, I thought of chasing after her. But my priority was finding out what had happened to Viv.

In the kitchen, Mrs Burman was staring at the policemen like they might have some sort of answer.

"Does Sanjay have any . . . enemies that you know of?" she asked, tentatively.

The bald one tried desperately not to smile. "Just his colleagues," he said. The fat one snorted loudly, then bit his fist.

"Look, Mrs Burman," said the bald one, trying to look like he was taking this all seriously when he clearly wasn't. "Your husband is not the, erm, hardest worker. We'll run this up the line, but we can't rule out the most likely possibility."

Mrs Burman looked up from her tissue: "What's that?" she asked, sniffing.

"That Mr Burman did all of this as an elaborate plan to get off work," replied the fat one, fighting the urge to laugh.

Mrs Burman was opening her mouth to protest when I stepped out from behind the door. "No! I know it's all true!" I cried. "And I know who did it!"

"Billy!" cried Mrs Burman. I rushed over and gave her a hug.

"It's my stepdad! Phil Pern! He's the mastermind behind all of this! He's a supervillain – they all are – and they're behind the plot! They are still planning on poisoning everyone at tomorrow's launch party! It's not the water that's being poisoned . . . it's the PholaCola!" The words rushed out of me like steam. When I'd finished, I was panting breathlessly.

The two policemen stared at me in silence for a moment. Then, in unison, they exploded in laughter.

"AHAHAHAHAHAHA!"

"OOHOOHOOHOOHOO!"

It went on for about a minute.

"AHAHAHAHAHAHA!"

"OOHOOHOOHOOHOO!"

When they'd finally finished laughing, they each wiped an eye. "That's gold, son!" said the fat one. "Absolute gold!"

"Phil Pern a supervillain! Glorious!" said the bald one.

Then they both lifted a can of PholaCola and each took a long slurp. The fat one finished his gulp and smacked his slobbery lips. "We should arrest that Phil Pern, then!" he chuckled. "For making such a delicious drink!"

The bald one's cheeks puffed out and he had to struggle not to spray PholaCola everywhere.

"Good one!" he said, fighting down his mouthful.

They both let out a long: "Woooooooooooooo." Wiped their eyes and stood up, pocketing their notebooks and popping on their helmets.

"Like I say, Mrs Burman. We'll, erm, run this up the line," said the bald one, then he gave his colleague a comradely slap on the back and they both turned to leave, slipping under the police tape and out into the street.

I turned to Mrs Burman. "I know it's true! I know it's Pheel who planned all this! And I'm going to get Viv back, I promise!"

She smiled, but I could tell that even she didn't believe me. "Just do *something*, Billy, please," she said.

If I stood any chance of convincing people and stopping Pheel, there was one thing I needed more than anything. And I had a horrible, horrible feeling I wouldn't find it.

"Can I go up to Viv's room?" I asked.

"Of course," said Mrs Burman, dabbing her eyes again.

I shot up the stairs and across the landing. Viv's room looked like an angry bull had been in it. I scanned the wreckage. There was no sign of the water pistol. They must have taken the serum. Connie's equipment was smashed and scattered across the floor. Close by lay a USB stick. I couldn't tell whether it was the one from Pheel's bat cave or if it had come out of the equipment. Maybe he had decoded the serum before they'd snatched him. I scooped it up and plugged it into his computer. It flashed, whirred, crunched and then a DISC CORRUPTED message flashed across the screen. My heart sank as I unplugged it and automatically slipped it into my pocket.

I crouched down and looked under the bed, hoping to find any sort of clue as to where they'd taken Viv. But there was nothing there. And that's when it hit me like a busload of elephants. There was one other thing missing. They hadn't just found the serum. They'd found the helmet and outfit as well!

When the realization hit me, it was like an icy fist had grabbed hold of my insides. They must think *Viv* was Bin Boy. I sat down and put my head in my hands.

I felt like I had been cut adrift at sea and was being sucked, helplessly, towards a gaping whirlpool that had already swallowed my best friend.

Viv was in unspeakable trouble.

Connie was a nervous wreck.

The L.O.V.E.R.S. had their serum back.

The Aphocalypse was nigh.

And there was nothing I could do about it.

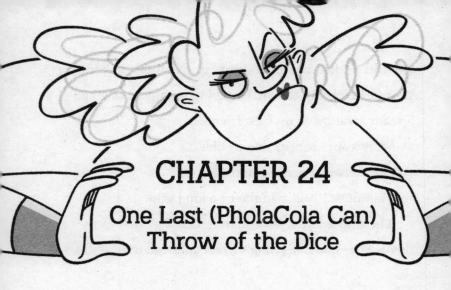

CHAPTER 24
One Last (PholaCola Can) Throw of the Dice

I didn't really sleep that night. Pheel was out building the launch party and all the henchmen were helping, so the Obserphatory was eerily quiet. I could see the preparations from my bedroom window. It was being held in the town park. There was a big stage and loads of screens and behind it all was the centrepiece – a model of a PholaCola Cherry can that was about the size of a small skyscraper. Henchmen marched around like little ants, as the light display warmed up – firing purples and blues into the morning twilight.

As the sun rose and the town slowly woke, oblivious

248

to Pheel's evil plan, I felt completely and utterly helpless. It was like I was standing paralysed on the tracks while a train sped towards me. There was only one more thing I could do; one more person I could try and convince. It was someone who always *used* to believe me. But now it was going to be a long shot.

The Obserphatory was deserted as I made my way down the stairs. Each footstep echoed around the marble walls. I stopped at the bottom and listened. Mum's squidgy work trainers squeaked busily around the kitchen. She was back from her night shift.

"Hello, sweetie!" she said, pulling open the fridge as I walked in. "Excited about tonight? Pheel has got us VIP tickets. We're going to arrive and leave by helicopter!"

I bet we were. To be whisked straight off to the Alps while the serum infected everyone. I gave a cursory look out of the window at the giant PholaCola can.

She took in my solemn face, the fridge gaping open behind her. "What's wrong?"

I took a deep breath and braced myself. "Mum, I need to tell you something. But this time I PROMISE, cross my heart and hope to die, that it is true. I wish I had some way of showing you, but. . ." As I spoke, my eyes wandered from Mum to the open fridge. Sitting beside the mayonnaise was the can of PholaCola Cherry that Pheel had left, with a note on it saying "DO NOT DRINK UNDER ANY CIRCUMSTANCES!" And that's when it hit me: I knew how I could prove everything to her!

"Whoa!" she said, ducking aside as I lurched past her, grabbing the can.

"I need to show you something," I said, then I took hold of her sleeve and pulled her through the kitchen. "Come on!"

"What's all this? Where are we going?" she said, as I dragged her out the kitchen door and down the winding steps that led to Pheel's zoo.

"It'll all make sense, Mum!"

We reached the entrance and I made a beeline for an animal enclosure. I dragged her along to the crocodile cage, but for some reason they weren't in there. Or maybe they were all underwater. In the next one, the man-eating wolves lay curled up in the morning shade, more like puppies than killer animals. They'd be perfect.

I turned to face her, took both her hands in mine and spoke breathlessly. "Mum, please, you have to believe me this time. What I'm about to say is the last chance we have to save the world."

"Billy. . ." she said, despairingly, but I cut her off.

"Pheel is behind the poison plot. He's put a poison inside PholaCola Cherry that is going to destroy all laughter. . ."

She tried to pull her hands free from mine but I gripped them harder.

"And that's why we are going to the Alps, to escape the horrible effects of the poison."

I paused for breath and she took the opportunity to yank her hands free, folding them across her chest. Her face looked like a storm cloud.

"Look, I know you don't believe me," I said. "But just watch."

I pulled a can from my pocket and cast my mind back to what a drop of poisoned condensation had done to Madame Mink's shawl. Then I shook the can as hard as I could and threw it into the enclosure like it was a grenade. The can hit the dried mud floor and exploded with a violent *POP!*, spraying jets of poisoned PholaCola Cherry over the helpless wolves. They whimpered and curled up tighter, tucking their muzzles into their bellies.

"Billy!" snapped Mum. "Just what do you think you are playing at?!"

"Just watch!" I said, hopping from foot to foot, waiting for the wolves to keel over and die. One of them yawned and another got up, circled around and then curled up again.

"Any second now, any second! Just watch! Come on!" I said, pleading with them to die like I've never pleaded with a man-eating wolf to die before. But nothing happened.

Every second that passed, I could sense Mum getting angrier and angrier. Her arms were folded tight and her foot tapped impatiently on the concrete floor.

Why wasn't the poison having any effect? "Maybe it takes longer with w—"

She snapped before I could finish. "I thought we'd got past this, Billy: this idea that Phil is a villain or whatever fantasy this is! He's not out to destroy your happiness! He's not out to destroy *anyone's* happiness! You sound . . . insane!"

She was red in the face now, and her eyes were glassy like she might cry if she wasn't so cross. I wound my head into my neck.

"I know he isn't your father! And he's not trying to replace him! But you need to remember what Dad said, just before he. . ." She trailed off briefly, before continuing with a fury that was dwindling into sorrow. "He asked you to look after me, didn't he? He said to make sure we were both happy, even if he wasn't there?"

She took a gulp and fought back a sob. "Well – this isn't making me happy! If you want me to choose between you and Phil, I'll always choose you, OK? But I shouldn't have to choose between being happy and being your mum."

And with that she burst into tears, turned and ran back towards the house.

"Mum!" I shouted. But it was no use. My chin sank down to my chest and I let out a long, loud sigh that turned into a howl of pure anger, frustration and sadness. Why did she have to bring Dad into it?

I was out of ideas. I had nowhere to turn.

When I finally felt like I'd screamed myself out, I looked down at Blemish, like a toy town bathed in long shadows of morning light. I looked past the rows of houses, past the school, past the giant PholaCola can and out to the little patch of green on the far side. If the world as we knew it was going to end tonight, there were only two people I wanted to spend the last day with. But unfortunately, one of them was mad with me, and the other was dead.

CHAPTER 25
The Mushy Chapter

I didn't go to school that day. I spent most of it sitting in Dad's graveyard. It was sunny and still. The grass was long and the daffodils we'd planted in his grave were just beginning to bud. He was as calm in death as he was in life. It was like I was in a leafy little sanctuary away from the chaos, disorder and imminent doom of the real world.

I don't want to go into Dad dying and all of that. But I'll just tell you he was a nurse like Mum and he died after a long illness.

I thought a lot that day. I thought about Dad. And I thought about what Mum had mentioned him saying.

I remembered vividly when he said it. When he was lying in his hospital bed, all thin and weak, I asked him: "Dad, are you scared?"

And he smiled and sat up, which seemed to take a monumental effort. "Only of one thing," he said. "Me not being able to fight in your and Mum's corner when I'm gone. It's up to you to look after her now. I want you both to be happy. Even if I'm not there." Then he gave me a big hug, his rib bones digging into my chest.

"Sure," I said, not really knowing how that would be possible, but my words were lost in his hospital scrubs.

I sat there for a long stretch of the afternoon, just thinking. I thought about how much scarier the world is when you lose a parent; how death and loss and grief can make you feel so helpless. I thought a lot about how I'd promised Dad that I would look after Mum. But how I was too scared and sad to even leave the house for a long time after he died. And I thought about what Connie had said: that real heroes don't set out to become heroes, they just do the right thing at the right time, even if it's really, really, really, really hard. I sat there and thought until I could hear the distant, excited sound of school finishing and the buzz of the launch party, which hovered like static over the town.

And then I stood up, kissed my dad's gravestone and set off across town.

CHAPTER 26

Help Me Be Bin Boy

I marched past Connie's gnomes with new-found purpose and knocked loudly on her door. When I'd sat in the graveyard, I hadn't just thought about Dad – I'd thought about why Connie had behaved the way she did at Viv's house. And I thought I had figured it out. She wasn't grounded. She wasn't confined to the basement. Something had made her scared of leaving that cellar.

Connie's dad opened the door with a soft smile. "She's downstairs as usual," he said.

I nodded, but stayed still. "Um, can I ask something first?"

"Of course, Billy," he replied, still smiling warmly.

I looked at my feet and braced myself to ask a question I couldn't believe hadn't occurred to me before. "Erm, where's Connie's mum?"

I glanced up to see his face change slowly from his usual pudgy smile into a look of soft sadness. "I'm afraid Billy that she, er, left," he replied. "When Connie was little."

"Does she ever see her?"

He shook his head. "I doubt she can even remember what she looks like. It didn't hit her hard until about two years ago. That's when she decided she didn't want to come out of the basement." Suddenly I understood Connie and the terrible pain of that loss. I could see why she hadn't wanted to go up those stairs and get hurt again. I knew that feeling too.

I crept softly into the cellar. She was in her usual position in the corner.

"Can you help me be Bin Boy again?" I said.

She turned with a face that was part startled, part happy and part embarrassed after her disappearance at Viv's house.

"You don't have to leave the cellar if you don't want

to," I added.

She shook her head, still wearing that scared look I'd seen at Viv's.

"I get it," I said. "I know your mum left. And I know how it feels to lose a parent. Your world is never going to be the same. And you want to hide, because you're scared of what that world might become. No one knows that more than me: I ended up with a supervillain for a stepdad! But hiding doesn't make it all better. So, you know –" I flicked my eyes skyward "– you should give it another go up there. And you don't have to be afraid, because you've got Viv and me now."

She nodded, like she recognized a truth in what I'd said but just needed some time to accept it, then mouthed a silent: "Thank you."

"That's if we can get him back and stop the Aphocalypse. . ." I said, scrunching up my face.

Her visage switched from fragile gratitude back to the fearless resolve of the Connie I'd first met. "We will. Pull up a chair." And I felt a little pang of adrenaline.

I scraped a metal stool over the floor and sat down as she said: "Tell me everything that you found out at

Viv's house."

I told her how Viv was kidnapped before he could decode the serum; how they'd stolen the sample back and mass-produced it for the launch party; and how they'd found the bin helmet under his bed. "They think *he's* Bin Boy," I said.

"That's terrible," she replied. Then she steepled her fingers and slipped into thought. "No, scratch that. It's not terrible . . . it's perfect!"

"What's so perfect about it?"

A mischievous grin spread across her face. "Because if Pheel thinks he has Bin Boy, then he won't be expecting him to turn up at the launch party. That means you still have the most important part of any plan."

"What's that?" I asked.

"The element of surprise!" She beamed, then stood up from her chair and picked up a remote control. "Come with me. I took the liberty of making you a few things."

She pressed a button and a set of metal doors slowly opened. A crack of yellow light broke out, then fanned across the floor.

"Whoa!" I said, my mouth falling open. "Is this for . . . me?"

"You betcha," she replied.

Staring back at me from the cupboard – like it was a suit of armour in a museum – was a shiny new Bin Boy costume. Except it wasn't an old white tracksuit and a bed sheet, but a PROPER superhero outfit. The clothing was silky and tight, and it had a long cape that shimmered in the light. In the middle of it all, sitting slap-bang on the chest, were the letters "BB" entwined together in a cool logo.

She walked over to the cupboard proudly. "It's flame proof, stab proof, bullet proof and chemical proof. And the helmet. . ."

I watched as she removed the helmet from the cupboard. I'd hardly even noticed it so far. But now that she held it, I could see it was so much slicker than the old plastic waste-paper basket I'd had on my head. Now, it was shaped like a shiny metal dustbin, with a pretend lid and handles and everything.

". . .is made from lightweight graphene – light as

a feather and super strong. Complete with inbuilt earpiece and . . ." She tapped the glass that now covered the eyeholes. ". . . it is completely sealed in. Meaning you're protected against any attempt to spray you with serum."

I gawped on as she replaced the helmet and picked up a gleaming pair of trainers.

"And, of course. . ." she continued. "A new pair of rocket shoes!"

I took them off her, practically dumbfounded. "This is amaaaazing!"

"You're welcome . . . teammate," she said.

I looked from the trainers up to her big, geeky grin and replied: "Thanks, teammate."

Her eyes twinkled with mischief. "I also made a few other little weapons – all non-lethal, of course. Perhaps you'd care to take a look?"

She pressed a button and another cupboard door opened. On three separate spotlit shelves sat a watch, a belt and a ring with two shiny green rocks on it.

"What do they do?" I asked, peering in closely.

"They tell the time, keep your trousers up and look

bling," she replied. "AND they help get you out of tricky situations. See this?" She picked up the watch, strapped it to her wrist and pointed it at a metal wastepaper bin sitting on the other side of the basement. "Get ready to duck," she said.

"Why?" I asked as she pressed a button on the watch. In a flash, the bin lifted off the floor and flew straight at us. I threw myself on to the ground as it whizzed past our heads and crashed into the wall behind us.

"What the. . .?"

"Supercharged neodymium," she replied, bouncing her eyebrows and looking pleased with herself. "The most powerful magnet known to man."

She slipped it from her wrist and on to mine. Then she fished the belt from the cupboard and wrapped it around her waist. She aimed at the battered bin and squeezed the buckle. A net flew from it and wrapped itself around the bin, sticking to it like slime.

"Gecko feet glue," she replied, looking even more pleased than before. "Harvested from tree branches in Mexico. Stickiest substance known to man. Anyone getting trapped in that net isn't untangling themselves this side of Christmas."

"Wow!" I replied, as she clipped it around my waist. I reached for the remaining green ring. "And what's this?"

She slapped my hand away. "Whoa, whoa, whoa! You don't want to manhandle this!" She removed it from the cupboard like it was a stick of dynamite. The emerald light of the stones danced on her face. "These are no normal stones. In fact, they're not stones at all. Each one is a single stink bomb made from the smelliest substance known to man."

I raised both eyebrows. "The smelliest substance known to man?"

"Yup. Pure, unadulterated skunk fart," she replied, slipping it on my finger. "Squeeze your fist and it will fire one stink bomb like a mini hand grenade. One sniff of it and you'll be having nightmares about it until you're ninety."

I looked at my new arsenal of gadgets and felt about three foot taller. If any of Pheel's supervillain buddies wanted to stop me, they were going to get netted and skunked.

"I better get kitted up," I said. "The launch party starts in an hour." She turned around while I slipped off my clothes, leaving them on her floor, and pulled on the Bin Boy suit. I could feel the excitement and adrenaline pumping through me as I pulled the white top over my head and buttoned the cape around my neck.

Connie turned around, gave an approving nod and said: "What's your plan?"

"I . . . um." I pulled a face. "I dunno." Plans were Viv's thing.

She blew out her cheeks. "Jeez. Lucky you've got me as a teammate. You're gonna need all the help you can get."

She pulled a chair up at her computers and furiously tapped some code into the blinking black screen. A load of CCTV screens popped up. I peered in closer and saw henchmen scurrying around.

"Whoa!" I said. "These are from the—"

"Launch party," she interjected. "Yup. CCTV backstage footage."

There were dozens of henchmen on each screen,

fixing lighting, pushing wheelie bins, cleaning the stage.

"Have you thought about how you're going to get in there?" she asked.

I gazed at the screen and shook my head slowly. I hadn't.

"Then it's lucky I'm here to help," she said, and pushed her finger against a wheelie bin on-screen. "These get emptied behind the bus depot next to the park. I saw it on CCTV earlier today. If you can jump into one when no one's looking, you'll be wheeled straight into the launch party." She flicked screens. "Right through this entrance."

I nodded and took a deep breath. "All right. Let's do it. . ." Suddenly, something caught my eye on-screen. It looked like two pieces of smashed glass at the bottom of a giant ladder. "What's that? Zoom in!"

Connie rolled her finger across the computer mouse. The smashed glass grew bigger and bigger on-screen until, with a jolt of electricity, I realized it wasn't just glass, but a pair of glasses! And not any old glasses!

"Those are Viv's glasses!" I cried. "I'd recognize them anywhere."

Connie was sitting upright now, bashing the keyboard to zoom out. "Where does that ladder go?" she said, flicking desperately through CCTV screens until she'd been through them all. "I can't find where it ends up! Wherever it is, there are no cameras!"

I peered in closer. The glasses were lying at the bottom of a vertical ladder strapped to the side of a gently curved purple wall. "I know exactly where it ends up," I said. "Zoom out further."

She flicked back to a wide shot of the launch party stage. "It's there," I said, pointing at the top of the giant PholaCola can. On it, I could make out two tiny dots. "They must be Viv and his dad. That's where they are keeping them."

"We need to get going, now!" I went to put on my helmet, then paused and looked at Connie. A thought suddenly hit me: "If it all goes wrong today, you'll be one of the only normal people left in this world."

She grinned and widened her eyes in mock horror. As she did so, her tinfoil hat slipped off her head and on to the floor.

I picked it up and handed it back to her. "I guess

that's kind of ironic," I said with a smile. "Seeing as you're the least normal person I know... In a good way!" I added.

She made a loud raspberry and laughed. "Whatever, Trevor! We're not so different, you and I."

"Oh, yeah?" I said, with a curious frown.

"Yeah. I hide behind my computer screens; you hide behind that costume."

I shrugged. Maybe I did.

"Any do you know why?" she asked.

"Tell me," I replied.

"Cos it feels good," she said. "It feels good to matter."

I stared at her as I let the words sink in. I *did* matter. I *was* doing the right thing. And I knew Dad would be proud of me. And that thought filled me with a strength and energy that a thousand supervillains couldn't destroy.

"Yeah," I said. "It feels awesome."

I smiled at her and she smiled back. Suddenly, we both realized we'd been staring at each other for way too long.

"Right ... yep," I said, clearing my throat and

looking at the floor.

"Okaaaaaay," said Connie, blushing and spinning around to her desk. "Stop being so cheesy and take this. It could make all the difference."

She pressed a button and her clenched mechanical arm extended from under her desk, slowly unfurling its fist to reveal a thin black stick.

I picked it up and raised an eyebrow. "A liquorice stick?"

She cocked a smile at me. "Never save the world on an empty stomach!"

CHAPTER 27
The Rescue Mission

The wheelie bin was pitch black and stank of old milk and wee. It juddered and shook, throwing me around like a stone in a washing machine.

Connie spoke down my earpiece: "Approaching launch party. Don't move a muscle. Over."

"Copy that." I said, as we went over a bump and my head was launched into the bin lid.

I could hear the roar of the crowd grow louder. It sounded like the whole town was there. Warm-up music blared out of the speakers, the bass reverberating through the bin.

"Show your passes!" barked a tinny voice from outside.

There was an excruciating pause, and then the words: "OK. Enter!"

"Jackpot," whispered Connie.

A set of gates creaked open.

We rattled some more and then, with a hollow bang, the bin crashed to a stop, throwing me to the floor. I lay there for a moment, as still as the bin. The bass, the roars and the clamour of the launch party all felt like a raging sea pounding at my little hidey-hole.

"When you're ready, Bin Boy," said Connie.

I cracked the lid open and peered out. I was backstage, all right. Barbed-wire fences towered over me and henchmen flowed left and right, carrying equipment and clipboards. About fifty yards away, I could see the base of the giant PholaCola can, and the silver glint of the ladder peeking out from its curved wall. Beneath a flowing black river of henchmen, I could see Viv's smashed glasses catch the light. Getting in the launch party had been one thing, but how was I going to get out of the wheelie bin without getting caught?

"OK, ready?" said Connie.

"For what?" I whispered.

"To make a dash for it!"

A siren cut through the backstage hubbub.

"FIRE IN ZONE C!" said a calm voice over the loudspeaker system. "ALL CREW REPORT IMMEDIATELY TO ZONE C!"

Suddenly, all the henchmen were running in one direction. Then, just like that, they were gone.

"Go! Go! Go!" she barked.

Like a flash, I was out of the wheelie bin and sprinting backstage to the ladder. The PholaCola can towered above me like an enormous purple tower.

"Up you go," said Connie.

I gulped down hard and pulled myself up, one rung at a time. Above me, the ladder shot upwards into the clouds, the side rails tapering together like train tracks vanishing into the sky. At one point, I made the mistake of looking down. My knees went momentarily weak. The ground dropped away below me – the bins now little dots – and I wasn't even halfway up.

"OK. Good news and bad news," said Connie.

"Give me the bad news," I replied, hauling myself up another rung.

"You're out of CCTV coverage. I'm losing visuals on you."

"Great," I muttered. Last time that had happened, I'd nearly drowned in a lake of serum. "What's the good news?"

"Erm..." She clicked her tongue in thought. "I'm still in your ear, I guess that's kinda good, right?"

I didn't have time to reply as I reached up for the last rung, took a breath, and peeked over the top of the can.

"Viv!" I cried. Relief poured out of me. I'd never been happier to see my best friend.

"Sourface!" whooped Connie.

He was sitting on a platform on the edge of the can, his bum on the floor and his hands fastened behind his back. His dad sat next to him, his hands also bound. Other than that, the giant can top was empty. Behind them, the heaving crowd stretched out in the evening sun, bouncing and rolling with every beat. It was a heaving, blaring, fun-packed festival that smelt of grilled burgers and cut grass.

"Bil..." he began to cry, then corrected himself. "Bin Boy!"

"Bin Boy!?" exclaimed his dad, before launching into a panicked garble. "I knew it couldn't have been Viv! I told them – 'It's just a fancy-dress costume you found in his room! He's not the real Bin Boy!'"

I hurried over to untie their hands, but not before I'd taken a second to peer over the edge. It was like we were on the tenth floor of a building. Directly below, beside the stage, was a vat of dark liquid that must have been PholaCola Cherry. My eyes wandered across the stage to a gallery where Mayor Blarblorn was seated slap-bang in the middle, his gold medallion gleaming in the afternoon sun. Not far from him, positioned on the front of the stage, were two long cylinders that looked exactly like a pair of cannons. One was pointed nonchalantly at the mayor's gallery and another at the crowd. I had a horrible feeling I knew what they were for.

"What's your plan?" whispered Viv as I picked at the knot tying his hands.

"Er, get you out of here, then stop Pheel?" I whispered back.

"No more details than that. . .?" replied Viv, but

he was cut off by the sound of the mayor taking the microphone.

"Nooooooow then!" he boomed. "Are you folks ready for the greatest party this town has ever seen?" The crowd roared. "Our host needs no introduction! He's the man who gave us PholaCola, PholaCola Lite and now all new PHOLACOLA CHERRY!! MR PHIL PERN!"

The noise of a helicopter cut through the screaming crowd.

CHOOKA CHOOKA CHOOKA

I squinted into the sun and recognized the sleek purple body immediately – it was Pheel's PholaCopter. Thirty thousand addicts reached up in greeting as it circled around and landed on a helipad above a clear glass cube.

Pheel stepped out and the screams reached a crescendo.

"Come on! We haven't got long," said Viv, jiggling his hands behind his back for me to untie them. But I couldn't pull my eyes from the helicopter. The Professor shuffled out after Pheel. Then, hot on his wheels, came

Mum. She looked overawed and gave a little wave to the crowd. There was no such shyness from Pheel. He was milking it, flapping his arms up in demand for more noise. The sound of the screams shook the giant PholaCola can. Mum was led into the glass cube by one of the henchmen, while Pheel picked up a mic and made his way to the stage.

"Hello, PholaCola fans!"

The crowd roared a response and he turned to the mayor's gallery.

"And thank you, Mayor Blarblorn! For my introduction and for letting us host the launch party here, in Blemish, the town I've always called home. And also, on a personal note, I want to thank you for always being so . . ." His words took on an edge as sharp as a razor. ". . . supportive. I hope you never lose your *fantastic* sense of humour."

The mayor raised his palms in mock modesty as Pheel gazed at him with an ice-cold smile.

In my ear, I could hear Connie saying: "Hurry up, Bin Boy! You've got bogies approaching the giant can." But I was too transfixed to register the urgency.

Phil turned back to the crowd and hollered: "Have you got your cups?"

The crowd lifted their hands as one, all of them clutching plastic cups.

"Good! Then in ten minutes you are going to get the world's first taste of PholaCola Cherry . . . when we spray you!" He gestured at the cannons and the crowd screamed. My worst fears were right.

I turned to Viv. "He's going to soak everyone in serum, isn't he?"

Viv nodded in knowing terror.

The camera was tight on him now – his whole face filling the giant screens. He looked over his sunglasses and I saw that same cold look he'd given me by the killer croc pen.

"And hello to our fans on every continent!" continued Pheel. "In Rio, Paris, New York, Mumbai, Beijing, Moscow and Sydney! I hope your launch party is as fun as ours!"

My fear turned to shock. "What does he mean?"

"I thought you knew," replied Viv. "They are holding launch parties at the same time all across the world!

They are connecting them all via live link!"

I looked down at the giant screens flanking the stage. They flicked through shots of the other launch parties and their crowds of roaring fans. A sinking feeling took hold.

"Connie, did you know about this?"

"No!" She sounded as shocked as me.

"It's hard enough stopping Pheel's evil plan in one place. How are we going to stop this happening on SIX DIFFERENT CONTINENTS?"

"First, you need to get off that can!" she replied. "And quickly! You've got henchmen coming!"

I untied Viv's hands. He shook them free of the rope and grabbed me by the shoulders. "You need to tell everyone what is about to happen! People will listen to Bin Boy! Get in front of one of these cameras and tell the world! Go, go! I'll free my dad!" he said, setting to work on his dad's ropes.

I moved for the ladder, but before I'd taken two steps, my heart stopped. A single hand appeared. It gripped hold of the rim and heaved itself up. The top of a head followed, then a face. It looked at me with blank, sinister eyes. I recognized him immediately. It was Henchman #1 – the same one who fallen into the serum. How was *he* still alive?

His dead eyes latched on to me and with barely a flicker of emotion he pointed at us and let out an almost inhuman cry.

Three more snarling henchmen heaved themselves over the rim, the last of whom was a terrifying man-giant. His eyes were grey – almost white – and he had a long scar running down the side of his bald head. Under his arm he held a box containing Lord Krung and his laptop. All four henchmen cracked their knuckles and took a menacing step towards us while Lord Krung's tinny speakers declared: "Bin Boy! We meet again."

"That's the person you want!" spluttered Mr Burman, pointing at me. "Not us! Leave us out of it."

"Get him!" exclaimed Lord Krung.

Down below, Pheel hollered into his mic: "ARE YOU READY TO PARTY!"

The crowd screamed back in unison as the first two henchmen charged at us.

"WHEN I SAY PARTY! YOU SAY PARTY!" hollered

Pheel. "PARTY!"

"PARTY!"

They were almost on top of us. Mr Burman let out a high-pitched squeal. Connie was yelling in my ear.

"PARTY!"

I gulped, grabbed my belt . . .

"PARTY!"

. . . and squeezed. The gecko net flew out of my buckle . . .

"CAN I GET A WOOP WOOP!"

. . . and wrapped itself around their bodies.

"WOOP WOOP!"

"ARGHHHHHH!" they screamed, falling to the floor in a tangled heap of limbs.

"Yes!" cried Viv, slightly prematurely.

"HARRRUMMMPHH!!!!!!"

The giant henchman's foot connected with my stomach. "Oooomp," I cried, as I flew backwards.

He dropped down on top of me, pinning my arms to the floor, his weight bearing down on my chest, squeezing the air from my lungs.

"Gerrrooff!" I croaked.

He let out a snort of derision, then reached up and grabbed hold of my helmet and twisted, then twisted some more, and some more... As my neck bent around to my shoulder, I realized he wasn't trying to take it off; he was trying to put me to sleep with a chokehold. The world started going dark and fuzzy. Stars fluttered before my eyes. I could hardly breathe. Connie was yelling something about farts in my ear. It took me a second to realize what she meant.

I reached out a weak fist and aimed it the best I could towards his face.

"Go ahead," he said, his baritone voice filled with derision. "Punch me, little Bin *Boy*."

With my last bit of energy, I wheezed at Viv and his dad: "Hold your noses!" and squeezed my fist. A soft POP sounded as the skunk bomb flew off my ring and fired straight into the giant henchman's laughing mouth. His face turned from sadistic delight into horror as green foam bubbled out of his lips.

"Arghhhhhhh!" he screamed as emerald clouds billowed from his mouth. Retching, he rolled off me.

I stood up and rolled my neck, trying to shake off the

pain and regain my balance. Somewhere from nearby, there was an annoying electronic voice.

"We'll get you, Bin Boy! This isn't the end! You can't beat the League of Villainry, Evil and Roboti—"

I reached down and closed Lord Krung's laptop.

"Oh ... shut up!" I said, rubbing my aching neck some more. Around our feet lay a mangled heap of henchmen, shrouded in green cloud.

"What's going on?" barked Connie.

"I just, erm, took care of them," I said, rubbing my neck while convincing myself that it had really happened.

She clapped her hands in celebration. "Nice one! Now get out of there!"

"To the ladder!" I said to Viv and his dad, who were still holding their breaths and wrapped in a terrified embrace.

Before I'd taken a step the green cloud part cleared to reveal a menacing silhouette. It was Henchman #1.

Oh ... farts. I'd forgotten about him.

His unblinking eyes and blank face barely twitched as he lifted a remote control with a big red button and mashed it with his opposing palm.

What the...? The section of the floor we were standing on began to pivot up. I felt my legs collapse and suddenly I was sliding towards the edge of the can. I desperately reached out and grabbed hold of the edge.

"Speak to me!" yelled Connie.

"We're going to fall!" I cried. Beside me, Viv and his dad clung on as desperately as me.

The floor levered higher and higher, until it was completely upright over the edge of the can and we were hanging on for dear life. Below us – a terrifying drop into the vat of PholaCola cherry. This is why Viv was up here! He wasn't being kept out of sight – it was an elaborate execution!

"Use your rocket shoes!" bellowed Connie.

Hanging on with just one arm, I leaned over and snatched for Viv's hand. "Grab hold of me!" I cried.

Viv's face was white. Trembling, he moved a hand towards me. But I could see his fingers slipping. His eyes bulged with terror. Then with an inevitable twang, the last one slid free and he was plummeting down, down, down.

"No!" screamed his dad, and dived after him.

"Noooo!" I shouted.

I had no choice. I took a deep breath and let go.

The wind whistled past my helmet and my stomach flew up as the vat of PholaCola cherry rushed towards me like an evil ocean.

CHAPTER 28
The Tank

SPLOSH!

I plunged feet first into the vat, shooting deep into the deadly black liquid.

"Viv! Mr Burman!" The scream escaped as harmless bubbles. I kicked and fought my way to the surface, breaking free of the black water and sucking in air.

"VIV!" I screamed. He didn't have my helmet and visor – he'd be drenched in serum!

"Over here!" he yelled. He was bobbing around behind me, his dad splashing next to him

"YOU'VE TOUCHED THE SERUM!" I cried.

"It's fine," he yelled, scooping some up in his hands

and slurping it. "It's not PholaCola! It's just water! The dark vat made it look black! We're fine!"

"Thank goodness. . ." I said.

Then Connie came into my ear: "Hang on, why were they planning on executing Bin Boy in a vat of *water*?"

On cue, a pair of dead eyes broke the surface. And another. And another.

I gazed deep into Dennis's cold eyes.

"Oh . . . *farts*," I muttered.

One by one, his crocodile friends gathered around him, their metallic grins glinting. I looked around desperately, but there was no escape from the sheer walls of the vat. We were trapped here with them. And Dennis looked like he was getting ready to attack. In a blur, he launched himself out of the water, his long green jaw wide open as he moved to lock his shiny teeth around Viv's head.

"ARRGHHHHHHHH!" cried Viv, screwing his eyes shut.

Instinctively, I whipped my watch out from the water and pressed it. Dennis swung wildly in mid-air, his snout stretching towards me like it was being pulled by an invisible rope until . . . SCHLUM! With a soft pop, his teeth flew out of his mouth and smacked on to my wrist.

For a second, they threatened to pull me under. I let go of the watch button and they slid off into the depths of the vat.

"Hahahahaha! Stop! It tickles!" cried Viv as Dennis's toothless jaws wrapped around his head.

The other crocs turned angrily towards me as they readied a revenge strike.

"Oh no you don't!" I muttered, and pressed my watch button.

Suddenly, they were all speeding towards me like logs being propelled through the water – their once-cold eyes now full of panic. And then. . .

SCHLUM!

SCHLUM!

SCHLUM!

SCHLUM!

SHCLUM!

Five pairs of platinum teeth flew on to my watch and sank into the black depths before. . .

WH**A**M!

I felt like my head was going to be ripped off.

"The last croc's on your helmet!" screamed Viv.

I could feel its vice-like grip trying to pull me under. Viv grabbed hold of my hand and desperately fought to keep me above water.

"Your ring!" yelled Connie.

She was right – I had a second skunk bomb on my ring. But to use it, I'd need to let go. I unfurled my fingers and felt my hand slip from Viv's.

The last thing I saw before I slipped under was Viv screaming: "No!"

I sank like a concrete block, the killer croc dragging me down, down into the shadowy vat. My lungs burning and my ears roaring with pain, I reached out behind my head, thrust my fist deep into the croc's throat and...

Suddenly, I was being propelled upwards on a cloud of green bubbles.

"Hold your noses!" I yelled as I broke the surface. A toxic green cloud broke around me, curling up over our heads and disappearing. Beside me, the motionless croc surfaced belly first.

"You're alive!" yelled Viv once he'd unclasped his nose.

"Thank heavens for that skunk fart, hey, Connie?" I said. Silence.

"Connie?" I repeated.

"Jeez, that's one puncture hole you've got in your helmet," said Viv.

I reached to the side and felt a dent by my ear.

It hadn't been enough to break the helmet's waterproof seal, but. . .

"Connie?" Still no reply.

It must have taken out my radio comms. I'd have to stop the Aphocalypse without her. I swallowed down any panic and reminded myself how I'd just KO'd those henchmen. I could do this.

From outside the vat, Pheel's voice still boomed.

"THREE MINUTES TILL YOU GUYS GET THE WORLD'S FIRST TASTE OF PHOLACOLA CHERRY!" he hollered. The crowd screamed some more.

"Quick," I cried to Viv and his dad. "Grab hold of me! We're going to fly out of here!"

They both wrestled a gummy croc from their heads and swam over, clutching hold of my arms. I moved my feet together underwater and tapped to activate the rocket shoes.

There was a faint fizz and nothing happened.

I tried again. Once more; nothing.

"They're not working under water!" I said. "Hold on so I can check."

I leaned back as they both supported me in the liquid and I lifted my shoes above the waterline. I clipped them together, and WOOOOSSHHHHHH! the flames blasted out.

"TWO MINUTES, CROWD! ARE YOU READY?!"

Then it hit me like a rhino driving a dump truck. I knew how to get us out of here AND save the crowd.

"Stand back!" I cried to Viv and his dad. Then I held my wrist against the wall and flicked the switch on my watch. With a soft CLINK it pinned to the wall like superglue. Then I leaned back, lifted my feet out of the water, pushed the soles into the tank wall and tapped.

WOOOOOOOOOSHHHHHHHHHH!!!!!!!

The rocket shoes fired. The sheer power of the jets

tried to send me flying backwards, but the watch clung to the tank walls, keeping me firmly in position. My arm felt like it might rip off as sparks sprayed like a Catherine wheel from my soles. The metal walls began to glow orange, and then red and then...

Suddenly I was spinning, twirling; desperately surfing a torrent of black water as the walls ruptured open and the contents of the tank spewed out – launching me across the stage and into the crowd in a big black wave. Everyone fell silent and the music stopped as I landed on a patch of soggy grass. Behind me, the torrent of water still gushed out and then... WOLLOP, WOLLOP, WOLLOP, WOLLOP, WOLLOP, WOLLOP, WOLLOP – seven crocodiles flew over my head and into the crowd like bowling balls.

The crowd were screaming again ... but this time, it was in sheer terror. And suddenly everyone was running, wildly stampeding towards the exit, chased by gummy crocs. Up in the gallery, the mayor was frantically pushing past women in a bid to escape.

Pheel was yelling pleadingly into the mic: "No! Don't

leave! Especially you, Ron. This is . . . erm . . . all part of the show!" But no one listened.

I staggered to my feet. Viv and his dad lay in a puddle next to me, dazed and confused.

I pulled them to their feet. "Go!" I said. "I've got this."

"But. . ." Viv began to say, but before he knew it, his dad was dragging him desperately towards the exits.

I turned to the stage. Quicker than a leopard on a deadline, the launch party had turned from tens of thousands of people, to just me, two supervillains and their henchmen. And I was the only person who could stop them.

"Bin Boy!" spat Pheel.

" G E E E E E E T T T T T T T T T HIIIIMMMMMMMMM!" shrieked the Professor.

CHAPTER 29
Aphocalypse Now!

Two henchmen launched themselves at me. The adrenaline kicked in. I tapped my feet together and, with the last blast of my rocket shoes, flew upwards, hearing but not seeing the dull thud of their heads bashing together. I arced over Pheel and the Professor and landed on the other side of the stage.

They spun around, venom in their eyes.

On the giant screens, I could see the global launch crowds watching us with shock and confusion. Through the speakers, the stunned murmur and chatter of hundreds of thousands of people mixed with the tinny beat of their party music. If I could just get to a TV camera, I could warn everyone about the serum. They wouldn't believe Billy Benbow, but they'd surely listen to Bin Boy?

"GET HIM!" bellowed Pheel.

I turned and dashed for the nearest camera. Two henchmen stood in my way. I squeezed my belt and took them down with a gecko net, vaulting their splayed, tangled limbs. Another henchman jumped out from nowhere and tried to clothesline me. I heard the snap of his arm as it broke against my helmet. From the other side of the stage, another one offloaded a round of bullets from his gun, but they just ricocheted from my outfit and flew back at him. He ducked and ran in fear.

I slid up to a camera and grabbed the lens.

"Everyone!" I cried. "Don't drink. . ."

"CUT THE CAMERAS!" shrieked the Professor. The camera drooped and its red light switched off.

I spun around desperately. Every other camera now lay limply on its stand. The remaining henchmen had either fled or were hiding from me. Only Pheel and the Professor remained, fuming at me from the wet, deserted stage.

Up in the rafters, a red light blinked. I squinted at it. It was a security camera! And it was still working!

I crossed my fingers. "CONNIE! IF YOU CAN HEAR ME, BROADCAST THIS FOOTAGE ACROSS THE WORLD!"

"What's he doing?" shrieked the Professor. "Why won't someone grab him?!"

I prayed Connie was listening.

"WORLD! YOU MUST LISTEN!" I cried. "EVERY DROP OF PHOLACOLA CHERRY IS POISONED! ANYONE WHO TRIES TO DRINK WILL HAVE THEIR MINDS ALTERED! IT WILL ERASE ALL LAUGHTER! IT'LL BE THE END OF THE WORLD AS WE KNOW IT!"

The global audiences fell silent. I could see their faces staring up at their own giant screens in silence. A sense of victory stirred in my stomach. Maybe, just maybe, it had worked! Connie had broadcast it across the world! The truth was finally out! The world knew that Pheel was an evil. . .

♫ NA NA, NA NA NA NA, NA NA NA, HEEEEY HEY ♫

On the screens, music erupted from every party, and the crowds exploded back into bouncy dance. My heart sank. They hadn't heard at all. Connie hadn't broadcast it. I stared into the CCTV camera despondently.

"Connie?"

But before I could say anything more, the wind rushed from my lungs and two giant arms wrapped around me.

"We have you now!" boomed a Russian voice.

Brenda the Immense stuffed me into the end of the cannon. The metal barrel pinned my arms tightly to my sides. I tried to wriggle free but couldn't budge.

"Leave his helmet on!" shouted the Professor from down on the puddled stage. "My henchmen tell me it is rigged with poison gas if you try to remove it. And who cares who he is? Soon, there'll be nothing left of him but a smear on some road!"

The Professor peered smugly up at me. Beside him, Pheel had changed into his purple Mr Pernicious costume. They were getting ready for the Aphocalypse.

I desperately scanned the glass cube for Mum, but

it was empty. Where was she? Had she run away with everyone else? I needed her more than ever. I needed her to see who Pheel really was!

"You thought you could outsmart us, eh, Bin Boy!" crowed the Professor. "Well, your efforts are coming to nothing!" He pointed at the screens, filled with an international cast of partying PholaCola fans. "Our party here was just the start! In a matter of minutes, the air shipments of PholaCola will reach these parties and you will be blasted out of this cannon to your death!"

I tried in vain to wriggle free. I tapped my rocket shoes together, but they fizzled and died.

A walkie-talkie crackled from the Professor's belt. "T-minus nine minutes to delivery."

"Marvellous!" crowed the Professor. "Let the Aphocalypse begin NOW! Brenda! Shake the can!"

Brenda nodded silently and walked over to the giant can of PholaCola. She pulled a lever and pistons hidden beneath it hissed, then began to move the can up and down, at first slowly, and then faster and faster.

"What are you doing?" I cried.

"Preparing to soak this town in serum, of course!"

301

he replied. "This is not stage decoration, boy! It is full of fizzy Cherry PholaCola! When Brenda releases the ring pull . . . WHOOSH!" He threw his hands up in a fountain motion. "The town will be soaked in delicious, cherry-flavoured PholaCola! It may sound fun, but I assure you . . ." He let out a dry cackle as his lips twisted into a wicked smile. ". . . it will be no laughing matter."

My eyes bulged. That was so outrageous it was almost unbelievable. Panic set in. Mum – where was Mum? She couldn't get soaked!

"Erm, Professor?" said Pheel, leaning into his ear. "Can we hold off on the giant-can plan for a few minutes? Just until I've tracked down my wife and stepson." He laughed nervously.

The Professor waved him away with a feeble hand. "We can't wait! This must happen NOW!"

Pheel suddenly looked flustered. "Just a few minutes. Fifteen, tops. Just so I can make sure they are safe." Then he added, almost pleadingly: "They mean a lot to me." I wasn't sure what I was more shocked about: a giant exploding can of poisoned pop, or Pheel saying I mean a lot to him.

The Professor spun to face Pheel. "You of all people should want this, Mr Pernicious!" he hissed. "Think how this town laughed at you for all those years! Look at that mayor and how he still laughs at you! Now is our chance. Revenge will be as sweet as cherry cola!"

Pheel was speaking slowly and forcefully now, with just a hint of desperation. "No! We must wait! If anyone deserves happiness – they do! Don't make me choose between this plan and them. Because I'll choose them every time."

Oh . . . farts, I thought, as my laser-focused hatred of Pheel momentarily wavered. I pushed the feeling back down and reminded myself of his evil plan.

The Professor's face was cold as ice. "We brought you on board because we thought you had a strong mind!" he spat. "You recognized what needed doing! So recognize this, Mr Pernicious – if we are to be taken seriously, we must act SERIOUSLY! No sentimentality must cloud our vision. Do you want to be a real supervillain or not?!"

Pheel face was half gripped with worry and half with anger. He grabbed the Professor by his lab coat.

"I said not yet! There's no point to any of this if they get infected. I want to protect them. I want all those snotty kids to stop laughing at Billy like they used to laugh at me!"

I screwed my eyes shut in frustration. *Oh . . . double farts!* If my hatred had been wavering before, it was now utterly confused. He wanted to end the world as we knew it . . . in order to protect *me*?! It was horrible and mad. But it was sort of a kind of nice gesture . . . I guess?

Pheel let go of the Professor's lapels and he fell weakly on to one knee.

"We're agreed, then," said Pheel, purposefully. "Fifteen minut. . ."

Before he could finish the sentence, he started shaking on the spot. What was happening? His whole body was reverberating, smoke rising out of his hair. Then, with one final convulsion, he slumped on to the floor, a crumpled smoking heap. With a wicked grin, the Professor tucked his cattle prod back inside his lab coat.

"Sometimes people need a little . . . prodding," he said, with a satisfied lick of his lips. "Brenda, tie him up as well! Mr Pernicious can no longer he trusted!"

Brenda marched over, lifted Pheel's body like it was a bag of crisps and bound it in rope. He sat – half-conscious, head drooping and groaning – with his back propped up against the giant can. Extraordinarily, I now felt sorry for the guy. It was all so confusing. I tried to shake my head clear and think of all the bad stuff he did. Like, in no particular order: trying too hard, looking at other mums, attempting to permanently erase the world's laughter. . . But then he was doing that last thing in order to look after me. Argh! It was such a brain scramble!

"Brenda, pop the ring pull! Explode this can!" snapped the Professor. His burly co-villain climbed into a white chemical suit. Then she slid the ladder around the giant can, gripped hold of a rung and began to heave herself up.

"As for you, Bin Boy!" He hit a big button at the base of the cannon and a countdown started.

"TWENTY . . . NINETEEN!"

"Soon you will be blasted into smithereens!"

The Professor rubbed his hands in glee. "Now, I should make my way into the helicopter! Mr Pernicious, so sorry you can't join us." Pheel groaned, his head still drooping. "Enjoy the Aphocalypse!"

With a cackle like a haunted house ride, he began to climb the ramp to the helipad.

Pheel shook his head and weakly tried to wriggle free. "Sally... Billy...!"

"EIGHTEEN ... SEVENTEEN ... SIXTEEN..."

Oh ... farts. I had sixteen seconds until I was launched into orbit and this town was soaked in serum. I fought and wriggled and squirmed until I was utterly exhausted. But I was squarely wedged in the cannon. Then, when I'd got my breath back, I fought and wriggled some more and then... *Whoooaaa! What was that?* The cannon suddenly swung to the right. It took me a second to work out what had happened. In all my wriggling, I must have pressed my watch button against the inside of the cannon. I did it again. The cannon swung again. My magnetic watch was moving the cannon!

"NINE ... EIGHT... SEVEN..."

Brenda was now halfway up the ladder. *If I could just...* I pressed my watch a little bit more. I swung right. Then I pressed it more gently. I edged right again. Then I pressed it softly once last time and the cannon nudged a tiny bit more so that it was pointing directly at the ladder.

"SIX ... FIVE ... FOUR..."

I drew in a deep breath. This was all or nothing. Either I was going to stop Brenda or I was going to end up in orbit.

"THREE ... TWO ... ONE..."

The cannon gurgled, then rumbled. I felt the PholaCola pressing up around my feet, trying to fire out. The pressure was building ... building ... I braced myself and then...

WOOOOOOOOOOOOSH!

CHAPTER 30

FSAve the Day

I arced through the air like a long white rocket. The world around me was a speeding blur, my tummy was somewhere back in the cannon and there was a smidgen of pee in in my pants. All the while, I was desperately praying that my guesswork was right. Because, if Brenda kept on climbing the ladder at the same speed, and I had pointed the cannon just right then. . .

OOOOOMPPHHHHHHH!

I smashed into Brenda like a cannonball into a bouncy castle. She let out a groan of pain and suddenly she was flying backwards, with me on top of her. We plummeted towards the stage, me surfing her like an inflatable elephant.

She looked up at me with a mixture of confusion, fear and anger...

"BIN BOY!" she screamed, streams of spit spraying against her suit visor. I held on to her for dear life as we fell, fell, fell. "I AM GOING TO K—"

With an ear-splitting crash, we landed on the stage. Her belly broke most of my fall, retracting in like a massive wobbly jelly and then bouncing me clear of her crater. I landed on the stage with a painful thud.

"Whoa..." I muttered, staggering up breathlessly to peer into Brenda's splintered crater. She lay motionless at the bottom, her arms and legs splayed out either side of her.

On the helipad, the chopper's propellers were spinning, ready for take-off, but the Professor wasn't on board. He was staggering furiously down the ramp, coming straight for me.

"BIN BOY!" he screamed in fury.

I might have saved the town for now, but it'd mean nothing if the rest of the world became infected. I had to find a camera and turn it on. I still had time to warn the other parties. I scrambled across the stage looking for one. I glanced over my shoulder, and the Professor suddenly seemed to have disappeared.

For a moment, I couldn't work out where he'd gone. Then his wrinkled hand appeared over the top of the cannon and he pulled himself up and into the firing seat. "I'M GOING TO BLAST YOU TO OBLIVION!" he screamed.

He pulled a trigger and a jet of PholaCola sprayed out, pummelling the stage. He swung it wildly towards me. I glanced from the cannon to the stage and momentarily froze. Before the jet hit me, it was going to pass directly over Pheel, soaking him in serum.

He was awake, and his eyes were wide in terror. "Professor! Professor! Please don't do this! I can't leave Sally and Billy all alone in this world!" His shrieks gave way to sobs. But the Professor didn't bat an eyelid.

I looked from Pheel to the camera. Then I looked from the camera to Pheel again.

"Oh . . . faaaaaaarts," I muttered. And before I knew it, I was running across the stage. With a split second to spare, I threw myself over him and covered us both with my cape. The jet stream of PholaCola Cherry pounded against the sides like a tent during a hurricane, but not a drop got through.

Oh, the irony. After all this, I was actually *saving* Pheel.

"Bin Boy ... thank you..." he mumbled, his face pressed against my helmet.

"Yeah ... well... You're welcome, I guess..." I muttered in reply.

"I made a mistake!" he continued. "I shouldn't have got sucked in by the Professor! I'm gonna change! I just wanna be a husband. A dad..."

"Stepdad," I muttered under my breath.

"I don't want to be a supervillain any more!"

I didn't bother to reply. I was too busy fighting to keep my cape over the both of us. Eventually, with a splutter and a gurgle, the jet weakened then finally stopped altogether. I peeked out. The Professor was still atop the cannon, its barrel dripping pathetically as he kept desperately pulling the trigger.

"FIRE! FIRE!" he yelled at it, furiously.

His walkie-talkie crackled. "T-minus one minute till air shipments reach their targets."

His fury slid away into a vicious laughter. "You may have saved this town for now, Bin Boy! But you haven't saved mankind! In just one minute, the world will be sipping on PholaCola Cherry. I win! You lose! There's nothing you can do about—"

DOINK!

The Professor stopped mid-sentence and slumped lifelessly forward in his chair.

What the. . .?

A figure in a chemical suit rose up behind him, holding a police nightstick.

"This way!" yelled the figure in a strangely recognizable voice.

More chemical suited figures swarmed on stage.

"We've got 'em now!" yelled the figure.

I did a double take. I knew exactly whose voice it was.

"Connie?!"

She pulled the helmet off of her chemical suit. "Just in the nick of time! Eh?"

From somewhere a voice boomed into a walkie-talkie: "Close all international airspace! Do not let anything land! This is a global emergency! And hose down this stage immediately!"

"Who . . . who are these people?" I muttered.

A tall man in a chemical suit strode up beside me and

flashed a badge. "FSA. Food Standards Agency. We have cause to believe that this substance is highly, highly toxic." I looked up at the screens; figures in chemical suits swarmed over every stage as the crowds emptied in panic. I slumped down on to the floor and took a deep breath. Then I looked again at the Professor's unconscious body. I ached with victory. We'd done it! We'd beaten the L.O.V.E.R.S.

The FSA man crouched down next to me. "On a personal note, Bin Boy... I don't suppose you could autograph this?" He held out a pen and I vacantly scribbled on a piece of paper. "For my kids, of course!" he added, with an embarrassed cough. "Thank you!" he said, beaming at the autograph with a bristle of his moustache.

"You're welcome," I replied, wearily.

He stood up and put his serious voice back on. "Right! To work, boys! Clean this mess up, pronto."

I looked up at Connie and gave her an exhausted smile of gratitude. "How did you...?"

She hopped off the cannon. "When I lost all visuals and comms with you, I went looking through the pockets of the trousers you'd left in my basement – to see if you'd taken your mobile phone with you. I dunno what I was going to do: Ring you? Track you? I was in a panic. But what I did find was this USB stick. . ." She held up the memory stick I'd found in Viv's room. "I plugged it in to take a look. It wasn't hard to fix. And when I did, I found an almost complete profile of the serum. Whether Viv knew it or not, he'd managed to crack it! I sent it straight to the FSA, who – with a little bit of creative hacking – thought I was one of their undercover agents!"

A passing agent in a chemical suit gave her a little salute and she casually returned it. "Carry on, Officer."

Connie looked super pleased with herself. "All I needed to do was lead the operation."

"You left the basement. . ." I said.

"Yeah," she said, overacting a shrug like it was no big deal. "To be a hero, sometimes you have to do things that are really, really, really, really hard."

I smiled. "Yeah, a wise person once told me that."

"And you know what makes it easier up here?" she continued.

"Rocket shoes?"

She grinned that maniac grin. "No, dummy. Friends."

A warm surge swept over me, but before I could say anything further, chemical-suited FSA agents swarmed all over the stage, mopping up the great puddles of PholaCola Cherry and taking samples. Phil sat sheepishly with his hands still bound, saying nothing. I almost – almost! – felt sorry for him.

But I had one last thing I needed to do. "Connie, can you do me a favour?"

"Sure!" she said.

I heaved myself off the floor, staggered to the edge of the stage and dropped down on to the grass where the FSA agents couldn't see me. She plopped down after me.

"What's this all about?" she said, as I slipped off my helmet.

CHAPTER 31
What a Hero!

As Connie slipped on the gloves, I heard a voice from onstage that I recognized in a heartbeat.

"Phil! Phil! What happened?"

It was Mum.

I hauled myself back onstage as Connie scampered into the shadows below.

"And Billy! I've been looking for you everywhere! Thank goodness you're safe!"

She had been running towards Pheel but diverted to me instead and pulled me into her chest. She hugged me till I thought I might pop.

"I ran into the crowd to try and find you when I

saw the crocodiles escape," she said, breathlessly. "But I couldn't find you and..."

She released me and held me in front of her, as if to double-check that I was in one piece.

"I was hiding by the side of the stage in a Portaloo," I said, spinning an elaborate lie.

"Thank heavens!" said Mum, then turned from me to Pheel and pulled his head into her chest. His hands were still bound behind his back, and I could see a little tear in the corner of his eye.

"Oh, Phil! I was worried I'd lost you. Not again. I can't lose another husband!" She began to cry, and Pheel's face crumpled like an origami punch bag.

"I'm sorry. I'm sorry," he sobbed. "This is all my fault."

She eyed his supervillain outfit suspiciously. "What are you wearing...?"

He fidgeted and tried his best to lie between blubs. "Just a ... costume for the ... erm ... launch party."

Mum let go of him and looked around at the FSA agents. Pheel carried on blubbing. Her voice took on an edge of sternness. "What happened here? How much trouble are you in?"

There was a long, pregnant silence. Pheel tried to compose himself to speak but he just kept sobbing and sobbing. As I watched him blub and thought about saying something, two paths seemed to open up in front of me. If I took the first one and told Mum and the police the truth – about the serum, the L.O.V.E.R.S. and their plan to erase laughter – Pheel would go to prison but Mum would be heartbroken all over again. If I took the other path, and kept schtum, Pheel would get off and I'd be stuck with him – maybe for ever – but Mum would be happy. I thought hard about what I wanted most in life, and in doing so, realized what the really, really, really, really hard thing I had to do was – and it wasn't stopping a league of psychotic supervillains destroying the world. I took a breath and spoke: "I can tell you. I saw everything from my hiding spot."

Pheel stared up at me, his eyes red and bloodshot. Then he looked down at the floor. He looked like the game was up. He looked beaten.

"What happened, sweetie? Tell me!" Mum's voice sounded panicky now, like she feared the worst.

I took a deep breath and cursed myself for what I was

about to do: "It was the Professor. He confessed to all of it. I heard him. He has been secretly plotting to poison everyone. Pheel just found out and tried to stop him. That's why the Professor tied him up."

Mum's panic evaporated like water on a frying pan and was replaced by pity for poor old Pheel's made-up plight. "Oh, Phil!" She hugged him again. "You trusted the Professor... How could he plot to do this to you?"

I looked away and scrunched up my face. I'd be lying to you if I said that wasn't really, really, really, really hard. I had come so close to exposing Pheel. But in the end, I'd wound up saving him to protect Mum. I guess he really did care about us. And while I didn't have to like it, I smiled at the thought that I'd kept my promise to Dad. Mum was safe. And she was loved.

A shout came from below the stage. "Hey!" I spun around to see Viv and his dad running towards us. "Billy! You're alive!" he shouted. "And Pheel and the Professor are under arrest!"

I beamed at my best friend. "Yeah, I'm alive! I saw the whole thing secretly. It's all the Professor. Pheel's innocent," I said, and gave him a wink. He frowned in confusion. I'd explain all later.

His dad stood next to him, surveying the scene. "We came back to look for Bin Boy!" he said, like a five-year-old studying the night sky for a glimpse of Father Christmas. "Did you know he saved us as well?!"

"What a hero," I said with a little smirk.

Behind Viv, hordes of people were now running towards the stage, cameras on shoulders and microphones in hand – news crews. Reporters quickly set up in front of the stage and began speaking into their cameras.

"Shocking events. . ." barked one.

"International incident. . ." boomed another.

"A PholaCola disaster!" shouted a third.

The mayor muscled his way through the crowd. "What a mess! What a mess!" he said, scratching his head in incredulity. "Phil Pern! I knew you'd mess up sooner or l—"

"OH, FOR HEAVEN'S SAKE, SHUT UP, RON, YOU HORRIBLE LITTLE BULLY!" cried Mum. The mayor stuttered and blinked in shock while Pheel mustered a little grateful smile through his sobs.

The moustached FSA agent who'd asked me for an autograph marched over and lifted Pheel to his feet. "Mr Pern, I'm afraid you're going to have to come with us for further questioning."

Dejected, he rose to his feet without argument, then fixed me with a pathetic but grateful look. "Thank you," he mouthed.

"Don't worry about it," I replied, fighting to hide a wry smile. "It's not the end of the world."

He did a double take as he was hauled off alongside the unconscious duo of the Professor and Brenda the Immense, who it took twelve agents to lift on to a stretcher.

The moustached FSA agent hovered beside me. "Young man, I hear you saw events here unfold? We'll need you to come in and make a statement."

"Of course," I said. "Anything to help."

He scribbled in his notebook and said, absently, "Thank you very much."

"You're welcome," I replied.

"Say!" He snapped up from his notebook and raised an eyebrow. "Your voice sounds very, very familiar. You're not Bin..."

"BIN BOY!" cried the crowd as one.

The noise of cameras furiously firing filled the air and everyone was suddenly staring and pointing at top of the giant PholaCola can.

There, towering above us, stood Bin Boy, his outfit gleaming white and his cape fluttering softly in the evening breeze.

Excitement rippled through the crowd like electricity. Flashbulbs burst; reporters gabbled breathlessly into their microphones.

"Early reports indicate that whatever happened here was largely thanks to the mysterious character who has become known as Bin Boy. . ."

"Bin Boy. . ."

"Bin Boy. . ."

His name bounced around the stage.

The mayor put his hands around his mouth and bellowed: "We owe you one, Bin Boy!"

On top of the giant can, Bin Boy put his hands on his hips and gazed out into the distance. Then he looked down and pointed straight at me.

Everyone spun towards me, cameras included.

What was Connie doing?? This wasn't part of the plan.

Then she lifted her hand to her forehead and gave me a salute. Blinking in surprise, I saluted back. Everyone looked at me in awe. And with a little tap of her replenished rocket shoes, she blasted off into the night sky like a comet.

"What a hero," muttered Mum, then looked down at me with bewilderment. "What was that salute all about? Do you know Bin Boy?"

"No," I replied with a casual shrug. "I just gave him a little bit of help earlier. Nothing much."

"Wow," said Mum, as if I had shaken hands with the Pope. "Well, you're *my* hero." Then she put her arm around my shoulders and squeezed me tight. "Come on, let's you and me go home."

"What about Pheel?" I asked.

She looked across at Pheel as he was loaded into the back of a police car, and then down at me. "You're safe. That's all that matters."

CHAPTER 32
Epilogue

I stared up at the billboard poster from the prison gates. It was about the size of a football field. "BIN BOY – THE MOVIE," it boomed at the top, beside a huge picture of some actor as Bin Boy.

I didn't think I'd ever get tired of staring at it.

"Shouldn't be long now," said Mum. I snapped to and took my eyes from the billboard. The gates loomed over us like a medieval castle.

"What time did you say Phil gets out?" I asked Mum.

She checked her watch. "Any minute now," she replied, then realized what I'd said and gave me a little smile. "Well done for saying his name correctly."

It'd been six months since the launch party and so much had happened. The world was a safer – although thirstier – place. Every drop of PholaCola in the world had been recalled, encased in cement and dropped in the middle of the ocean. People had got pretty sick from the withdrawal symptoms. They even had to close school for a fortnight. I heard Brayden Balls was so ill he pooped himself in the middle of a supermarket. But seeing as Viv, Connie, Mum and me were pretty much the only people not to be affected, we had a great time hanging out! Connie was out of the cellar for good and being just as mad and brilliant and hilarious in the outside world as she was underground.

The Professor and Brenda the Immense were both locked up for life. But the rest of the L.O.V.E.R.S. were never implicated and had gone underground – at least as far as I could tell.

Thanks in part to my testimony, Phil escaped with just a six-month prison sentence for supposedly failing to implement enough safety checks and spot the Professor's evil plot. But no one ever knew just how deeply he was involved. Of course, PholaCola went bust and he lost all of his money – his accountants had to sell the rocket cars, the crocodiles, the volcano, even the Obserphatory, which was just fine by me – Mum and I moved back into our old house while he was in prison. We hung out together, played Scrabble, and had fun with just the two of us. It was like old times.

It's lovely to visit the past now and then. But you can't live there, otherwise you'd never change. A few weeks ago, I suggested to Mum that we sell it and look for somewhere that doesn't remind me of Dad every moment. She smiled and said, "He'll always live with you up here," then placed her hand on top of my head.

As for Bin Boy: movies aside, he hasn't been seen since the launch party. Which means that, with every day that goes past, my supposed meeting with him gets more and more legendary. People just can't get over how cool it was that I helped him. That he saluted *me*! My coolness levels have gone through the roof at school. Even Brayden Balls keeps giving me sweets in return for getting Bin Boy's autograph, so that he can sell it or eat it or whatever he does with autographs.

"DOORS UNLOCKED!" barked a guard on the other side of the gates.

They creaked open. And there on the other side was Phil. He looked thinner, and his normally immaculate red hair and beard were dishevelled. For pretty much the first time ever, he wasn't wearing a purple suit but some blue jeans and a white shirt that were about three sizes too big. And for the first time ever, I didn't feel unadulterated hatred at the sight of him. In fact, I'd even describe it as ... well, if not happiness, then let's say tolerance.

He looked half overjoyed, half relieved. Mum ran forward and hugged him. I sauntered forward and patted him on the back. He grabbed me and pulled me in for a hug that lasted about ten seconds too long. He smelt of a charity shop.

Mum let go of him and broke the bad news – "We had to sell the Obserphatory –" before trying to put a positive spin on it "– but we've got a new home!"

He didn't flinch at the news. "I don't need a big home or flash cars or lots of money. I just need you guys."

He moved to put his hands around our shoulders and

I decided to let him. "Come on, let's have a do-over," he said, and we set off down the pavement.

He looked from Mum to me and smiled. Mum rested her head on his shoulder. And, at that moment, I didn't mind smiling back. I guess sometimes you have got to be brave enough to do the right thing, however hard it is. And because I loved Mum so much, this felt right. When we were huddled under the cape together, Phil promised me he'd change. He just wanted to be a good husband. A good (blurgh!) stepdad. And, at that exact moment, I let myself believe him.

We walked on in silence for a bit. Just before we reached the corner, Phil looked down again and smiled, first at me, then at Mum; then he looked up and flashed the briefest of smiles at a purple car. I glanced across to see if I'd dreamt it, but the car disappeared around a corner. The only thing I saw, staring back at me from the rear window, was the glistening eyes and black fur of a mink.

ACKNOWLEDGEMENTS

My everlasting thanks to:

My A-list agent Chloe Seager for believing in Bin Boy from the very beginning and seeing everything that was good – and everything that could be better – in Billy's story. My brilliant editor, Yasmin Morrissey, for your incredible passion for the book and your unashamed girl-crush on Connie. The rest of the Scholastic team, for welcoming me with such wide arms and making Bin Boy a reality: Lauren, Harriet, Peter, Liam, Bec and Georgina, to name just a few. Emma McCann, for drawing Billy, Pheel, Viv, Connie and the L.O.V.E.R.S. even better than I had imagined them. Lou Kuenzler at City Lit for teaching me what a story actually is and for giving me the encouragement to go and write one. Every City Lit member who ever gave me feedback - all of it, good and bad, was priceless. Mum, for a lifetime encouraging my reading and writing. And Dad, for the same – my only regret is that you aren't here to see where it has led. And finally to Issy, for your absolute, unwavering belief in me.